PART ONE

Chapter One

Poppy watched the aeroplane back slowly off its stand. It looked like an elephant taking care not to squash anything smaller. Around it buzzed vans with flashing lights and men with flashing signals. Somewhere inside the plane's great belly sat her mum, on her way to Poland.

Poppy stared at the little round portholes, knowing there was no way she could see her mother's pale and anxious face. She thought: now I'm an orphan.

'You're almost an orphan!' exclaimed Poppy's best friend Jude, who was standing at her side.

Poppy swung round. 'They're not dead, you know.' It was annoying that Jude had guessed her secret thought.

'With your dad in prison and your mum in Poland, they might as well be dead.'

'You're supposed to be my friend!' Poppy felt tears at the back of her eyes ready to pop out at any moment; arguing might hold them back.

'But you're more like a slimy witch.'

'Well, you're like a frizzy red-headed hobgoblin.' They were hissing at each other like fighting cats.

'Whatever's the matter?' Jude's mum, who'd driven them to the airport, stared at them. 'You're not even watching the plane take off, which is the whole point of our being here.'

All three turned round to watch the plane lumber into the sky and then sweep gracefully upwards,

'Sorry,' mumbled Poppy – and burst into tears.

'Sorry. Sorry. Sorry.' Jude flung her arms round her: 'I'm so mean.'

'Three fairy cakes,' Jude's mum opened her paper bag. 'First come, first served.'

Poppy stopped crying, took the biggest, most glittery cake and tried to stop that word 'orphan' repeating in her head.

In the car driving back to London, Poppy, who was sitting in the front, decided that Jude was always at her worst when things were bad. Nothing bad had ever happened to her. Two years earlier, when Poppy's dad had first gone into prison, Jude had been horrible, mocking and cruel. Poppy had thought she'd never forgive her, but she had done, and now she was going to stay with her while Irena

(Poppy's mum) was in Poland. In good times, they had lots of fun together.

'Your mum will be home in a couple of weeks,' said Jude's mother kindly, 'once your granny's back on her feet.'

'She's very ill,' said Poppy doubtfully. 'Mum told me she can't even speak.'

'She's had a heart attack,' announced Jude from the back seat. She was using what Poppy thought of as her 'doom-laden' voice. Of course, it was always used about other people's doom.

'I'm sure she'll soon be better,' said Jude's mother firmly, and Poppy saw her frown at her daughter in the rear-view mirror.

Even without Jude's determination to make the worst of things, Poppy would have found it hard living with her. The house was certainly big enough – she was sleeping in the bedroom belonging to Ben, one of Jude's older brothers who was away at university. She knew the family well; their dad was an Italian chef who owned three restaurants and was hardly ever around. So it was Sally, Jude's mum, she saw most of. She didn't work like all the other mums Poppy knew – Poppy's mother was a piano teacher – so she had plenty of time to bake cakes and make the house look pretty and lay out their clothes in neat piles.

Poppy knew she was lucky to be staying in such a comfortable, friendly place. There had been a terrible moment when her mum had threatened to take her to Poland, not a good idea since Poppy didn't speak a word of Polish. Poppy should have been happy, but she wasn't. Everything felt just too strange, partly because it had all happened so unexpectedly.

As soon as they got back from the airport, Poppy pretended she had a headache and went upstairs and lay down on her new bed.

Jude stood at the door. 'It's not very girly in here. Wouldn't you rather come in with me?'

It was true – the walls were covered with posters of cricket teams and angry-looking racing cars. 'Your mum thinks we'd keep each other awake all night chatting.'

'It smells, too. My mum says boys start smelling when they're about fourteen and don't stop till they get married.'

'I don't mind,' muttered Poppy, wishing Jude would go. 'Angel and Will don't smell.'

'They're not fourteen, are they?'

Realising she wasn't going to get much from Poppy,

Jude went off. In a few minutes Poppy heard her out in the garden shouting at her other brother, Rico. By the way her voice came in waves, Poppy guessed she was jumping up and down on the big trampoline. It was a good way to spend a Saturday afternoon in the summer and she wished she felt like bouncing too.

Instead, she thought about Will and Angel. They were her two friends who were boys, and very different from each other. Will, although clever and adventurous, was often weak and sickly, while Angel was witty and a natural rule-breaker who seemed to spend more time on the streets than at home. His dad had been in prison with Poppy's dad, Big Frank. They'd met when they'd both been visiting their dads.

Thinking about Angel made Poppy realise she hadn't seen him for weeks. He always made life seem more exciting, if a little scary sometimes. Suddenly restless, Poppy swung her legs off the bed and crept to the edge of the stairs. A delicious smell was coming from the kitchen; Jude's mum had once been a professional cook like her husband.

But she's not *my* mum, thought Poppy, and this isn't *my* home. Slowly she began to creep down the stairs. That's what she'd do: go back to her own home.

It was only two streets away and she wouldn't stay long – just long enough to feel she wasn't an orphan.

The shadows were lengthening as Poppy walked along the street. She looked up at the blue sky and felt free for the first time since saying goodbye to Irena. In a few days' time the summer term would start – typical, just when the weather was turning nice.

Poppy shook her mop of red-gold curls so that they glinted in the sun and began to run as fast as she could. Feeling free made her think of her dad, Big Frank, locked up in prison. He'd been such a free sort of person, always making people laugh with his silly jokes. At first she couldn't believe he was guilty of drug smuggling. This was serious. But then he himself had told her he was guilty. It had been a horrible shock, but in the end she'd managed to forgive him and love him despite everything. That was old news. She could cope with that now.

Poppy arrived panting at the house where she and her mother lived on the bottom two floors. She'd only left that morning, but now she felt like a burglar because her mum had told her to stay away. 'I want you to feel settled with Jude and her family,' she'd said, almost in tears. As per usual.

But I'm not settled, thought Poppy, taking out

the key she'd kept hidden away. And all I'm going to do is pop in for a moment to make me feel calmer.

With her heart beating a little too fast because she didn't usually disobey her mum and because it seemed weird being here on her own, Poppy turned the key and opened the door. Light came in from the landing, falling brightly on the carpet at the bottom of the stairs.

Something on the floor caught Poppy's eye. She took another step forward and saw, quite clearly, two round red spots. She took another step and saw another spot by the door to the kitchen.

They were the brilliant red of fresh blood.

Slowly she walked forward and pushed open the door. It was darker inside because her mum had drawn the curtains before she left. She peered around but the room seemed empty. Perhaps she was imagining things. Then she saw two more spots by her feet.

'Hello!' Her voice wavered. She felt brave not running away.

'Poppy?' Despite her being so brave, the whispering voice nearly made her jump out of her skin.

'Who is it?'

'It's me. Angel. I need help.'

Chapter Two

'Angel.' Of course, it would be Angel.

'Where are you? I can't see you.'

'I'm under the table. I didn't know who was coming in, did I.'

Poppy watched nervously as Angel crawled out and stood up. He was cradling one arm with the other. Something dripped on to the floor.

'You're bleeding!' Poppy could hear she sounded more accusing than sympathetic.

'Yeah. Worried about your mum's clean floor?'

'My mum's in Poland. My grandmama is very ill.'

'Sorry.'

Poppy suddenly saw that Angel's habitual nonchalant slouch was even lower than usual. In fact, he looked as if he might faint.

'Here. Sit down.' She pushed a chair towards him.

He sat down, hanging his head so that his thick black hair hid his face.

'You frightened me,' said Poppy. 'How did you get

in anyway?'

'Toilet window,' Angel's voice was very low. 'Had to break it a bit. Sorry.'

'Is that how you cut your arm?'

There was a long pause, then a muttered, 'Maybe.'

'I'd better get you a plaster. I can't stay long because I'm staying at Jude's and I just sort of slipped out.'

Angel didn't answer. Poppy went upstairs to the bathroom and found some disinfectant and a box of plasters. On the way down, she thought it was odd that Angel had wanted to see her badly enough to break a window. Even if his mum was busy with two little kids and a husband whose second home seemed to be prison, surely she could have given him a plaster.

Poppy came back into the kitchen and automatically reached for the light switch.

'Leave that off!'

Surprised, Poppy stared at him. 'How can I see what I'm doing if it's pitch black?'

'OK,' said Angel reluctantly, 'but leave the curtains.'

'It's the right arm, isn't it?' Poppy crouched down beside him.

'Yeah. I wound some toilet paper round it. It'd stopped bleeding – started again when I was climbing.'

'I thought you said you did it coming in through the window.'

'I said maybe. Made it worse, didn't I.'

Poppy bent over the arm and immediately realised why there were drips. The whole arm seemed to be a sodden mass of red paper. She gulped. Blood had never been her thing.

'Go on,' urged Angel through gritted teeth. 'Can't you see it hurts?'

Half-shutting her eyes, Poppy unwound the paper and dropped it on the floor. She'd never known that blood smelled before.

'You've got a long-sleeved T-shirt on.' Poppy sat back on her heels and put her bloody hand to her head. She thought she might faint. 'You've got a hole in your arm!' she whispered, horror-struck.

'I know. I know. Do you think I don't know?'

'You need a doctor. A hospital. A & E. That's where Mum took me when I fell off a wall.'

'I can't. That's why I've come to you.' Angel's voice was shaking and Poppy had a horrid feeling that he might be about to cry, which was scarier than anything because Angel never cried. He was so cool, he was like an iceberg.

'What do you mean, can't? I can't stick a plaster over that. It's a great big gaping wound. It needs stitches. And what about your T-shirt? How do we get that off?' Poppy was getting angry. Also, she was beginning to worry about being missed at Jude's.

'Can't tell you why I can't. But I can't. Just can't. Cut off the T. It's ruined, anyway. I'd do it myself, if I wasn't right-handed.' Angel's whole body was shaking now.

'I'll call 999 on my mobile.' It was like a nightmare or a scene from a movie – the sort of movie she didn't want to watch.

'If you do that, I'll run away!' Angel tottered to his feet and more blood spattered down.

'All right. All right.' Poppy hurried to the kitchen cupboard and found a pair of scissors. 'I'd better get a bandage.' She ran upstairs and was soon down again.

'I'm still here.'

'It's no good being impatient.' Cutting off the T-shirt was the worst thing Poppy had ever done, with Angel flinching and gulping and even swearing once, which he never did, at least, not in front of her.

Poppy's mum said 'Our Lady', blushed every time someone swore and, if it was a child, a tear trickled out of her eye.

'This stuff won't cut.'

'Do it, man.' Angel was speaking through gritted teeth and his eyes were shut.

'In films, when they do this kind of thing, it takes a second,' muttered Poppy.

'Not a film.'

At last Poppy had cut off most of the sleeve.

'The next bit will hurt.' Her mum always warned her before she put on disinfectant.

'As if the first bit didn't.'

Carefully, Poppy diluted the disinfectant in a bowl, then found a clean cloth. She wished her mum was there. The strong smell filled the air as Poppy squeezed it over the wound.

'Owhh! Ohhh! Owhh!,' shrieked Angel.

Poppy decided not to say *I told you so*. 'Sorry.'

'Just bandage it.'

Finding her hands were now shaking, Poppy did this as well as she could, although it all looked a bit of a bundle. It was a relief, however, not to see the wound any more.

'That's better.'

'Um. Thanks. Ever thought of taking up nursing?' For the first time, Angel seemed more like his usual perky self.

'I'll put on the kettle,' said Poppy, feeling a bit like her mum. 'Then I'll clear up.'

Clearing up consisted of shoving the bloody tissue and bits of T-shirt into a plastic bag, then wiping the floor with a wet cloth before disposing of it in the plastic bag. 'I'll put it all in the bin before I go. It gets emptied on Monday.'

Cheered by her efficiency, Poppy sat down with Angel and two mugs of instant soup. Suddenly she looked at her watch. 'It's nearly half-past six!'

'So?'

'Jude's mum will be going mad.'

'So?' Angel looked down at his steaming mug.

Poppy jumped up. 'I've got to go. Come on.'

'And leave this great soup?' Angel bent lower over his mug.

'What's the matter with you?' Poppy was really panicky now.

'Can I stay? Just for a bit.'

Poppy stopped at the door. 'Oh, Angel. Why don't you go home?'

'My dad's there, making trouble. Sometimes I wish

he'd go right back into prison and stay there. And my mum's going to have another baby, isn't she.'

'But she'll need you to look after Seraphina and Gabriel.'

'She's got her sister there. Eloise.' He made the name sound like a threat.

Poppy could see there wouldn't be much room for Angel in what she'd always imagined as a small flat, although Angel had never invited her there. All the same, she sensed Angel wasn't telling her the real reason for wanting to stay where he was.

'Can I hang out here till tomorrow?'

'Tomorrow!'

'Then you could come over and get the key. Or you can lock me in if you like.'

Poppy took a few steps back into the room. 'You're in trouble, aren't you? That cut. You still haven't told me how you got it. You don't want to hang out here, do you? You want to hide here?' Poppy glanced up. 'With the curtains drawn. What's happened, Angel?'

'You don't want to know, I'm telling you. Just let me stay here tonight. I'm safe here.'

'Safe! What do you mean, safe?'

'Why don't you just go!'

'Tell me.' Poppy stood and stared at Angel;

she saw he had begun to shake again.

'OK. You want to know the truth.' Angel's voice was fierce but trembling, too. 'Real story. That cut's done with a knife. I was in a fight and someone pulled a knife on me and after, he cut me; I gave him a push backwards and he tripped on the kerb and fell backwards and hit his stupid head and lay there flat out. And, for all I know, he might be dead because I ran then. So you can see why I can't go to hospital and you can see why I want to hide here, because the Flyers will be after me!'

Chapter Three

Poppy had a strong urge to run out of the door and leave Angel to get on with his own problems. Surely it was enough to have a dad in prison and a mum in Poland – to be an 'orphan', as Jude put it? She pictured Jude bouncing and carefree in the sunny garden while her mum baked in the kitchen. Then, just as quickly, she found herself swinging in exactly the opposite direction.

She didn't mind if Jude and her mum were worried about her. It would do them no harm to have a few worries. Angel needed her here and now. It felt good to be the one who was needed, not the needy one. She went over and sat down.

'I don't understand the bit about not going to A & E.'

'What about Jude?'

'She'll survive.' Poppy picked up her soup again and sat back to listen.

'I've got friends, haven't I. I need them when

my flat's like rush hour all the time. Know what I mean?'

'Yes,' said Poppy, to encourage him. She tried to imagine a flat like rush hour. She and her mum had had the quietest life imaginable since her dad left. 'What sort of friends?'

'Brothers. Big brothers. We got up to things.' Angel finished his soup with a gulp. 'At least, they got up to things and I waited outside. I didn't think much about it. Like I was pleased they wanted me in.'

'Stealing?' asked Poppy, trying not to sound disapproving, because that wouldn't help.

'Supermarkets are stealing from us, aren't they?' said Angel self-righteously. 'They make billions, don't they, while we starve.'

'You're not starving,' pointed out Poppy.

Angel ignored this. 'It's not like the local corner shop. I'd never get involved in that. Anyway, I was only standing outside and it was fine. They walked out with a bottle of vodka. Disgusting, it was.'

'You didn't try some!'

'Disgusting, I told you. Soup's better.'

'So how did you get into a fight?' Despite her decision to let Jude stew, Poppy glanced at her watch.

Angel's head went down again. 'My arm hurts,' he muttered. 'I need to rest, not be interrogated. It's like being picked up by the feds.'

'So why can't you go to hospital?'

'Because they'd know it's a knife wound and they'd call my mum and she'd tell my dad and he would go mad...'

'I thought your dad was always in trouble,' interrupted Poppy.

'Doesn't mean he wants me to go the same way. Means he knows the signals, though.'

'Like being in a gang?'

'Brothers. There's nothing wrong with brothers.' Angel settled down into glumness again. 'The hospital would call the police, too. Seeing as it's a stab wound. But that's not the worst of it. Not my dad nor the feds.'

'What is it, then?'

'The bro who fell down and didn't get up. The Flyers'll be out looking for me, won't they?'

Now Poppy understood. 'You mean, you think these friends called 'Flyers' are after you to get revenge.'

'Revenge. Yeah. That's it. Good word.'

'So that's why you're hiding and want the

curtains drawn.'

'Got it!' He looked up at her, his dark eyes bright and hopeful. 'Let me stay here tonight. Then tomorrow you can come in and let me out. We're mates, aren't we? It's what you do for mates.'

'Your mates seem keener on sticking knives in,' said Poppy and she thought that Angel could perfectly well climb in and out of the window he'd broken any time he pleased.

'If you don't care...' Angel jumped up, then gave a shriek of pain as his arm knocked the table.

'All right.' How could she help feeling sorry for him? 'There're packets and tins of food in the cupboard. Now, I've got to go.'

Angel sank back down into the chair. 'Cheers.'

Poppy hurried to the door. She turned briefly, 'See you in the morning.' Angel raised his good arm, but his eyes had closed.

It seemed very bright outside, even though the sun was about to drop behind the rooftops. Poppy blinked as her eyes adjusted from the dark kitchen. It was hard to believe the strange scene she'd left: Angel hiding under the table, his bloody arm, his frightening story. But it was real enough, because why else would she be dropping this bag of revolting stuff in the dustbin?

She knew she should get a move on, but instead she walked slowly, trying to take in what Angel had told her. She was so deep in thought that at first she didn't hear her name being called.

'Poppy! Poppy!'

She looked up and saw Jude and her brother Rico racing towards her, shouting. Jude arrived at her side panting.

'Wherever have you been? We've all been out looking. Mum's about to call the police. I thought you'd been kidnapped!'

'Slow down, Jude,' said Rico. His voice was deep and manly-sounding, even though he was only fifteen. 'Give her a chance. The poor girl looks like she's had a shock.'

'I'm fine,' said Poppy as brightly as she could. The truth was that the sight of Rico's kind face and solid form made her want to burst into tears. 'I just went for a walk,' she murmured. 'Sorry.'

'But you were gone for ages!' persisted Jude. 'Where did you go?'

'Nowhere,' answered Poppy, so miserably that

Rico put his arm round her shoulders.

'Come on. Let's go and eat that pie I've been smelling in the kitchen all afternoon.'

Jude gave up, and they walked down the street together arm in arm. Poppy knew Jude hadn't finished with her questions, but at least she had time to think how to answer them. Angel hadn't actually told her not to talk to anyone.

That evening everyone was very nice to Poppy. Jude's mum had decided that Poppy had been feeling sad because her mum had gone away to Poland and she had run off to be alone. Which was, of course, the reason Poppy had left the house in the first place, although, since meeting Angel, she hadn't thought of her mum or dad once. She was far too worried about Angel.

'Do you want to share rooms tonight?' whispered Jude as they went upstairs to bed.

Poppy thought of Angel all alone in her house with that horrible wound. How lucky she was to have a friend like Jude!

'Yes,' she whispered, 'Will your mum mind?'

'Course not. It's Saturday, and we don't start school till Tuesday.'

Upstairs in the dimly-lit bedroom. Poppy could see Jude lying on the camp bed she'd insisted on taking so that Poppy could be comfortable in her bed. Where was Angel sleeping? Poppy wondered.

Both girls were wide awake.

'Where did you really go this afternoon?' whispered Jude. 'I was so worried. And you looked so funny when we found you. Like you'd seen a ghost.'

'I went home,' said Poppy slowly.

'Then what? What happened? I won't tell anybody, I promise.'

Poppy turned restlessly. She really needed to share the secret or she'd never get to sleep, imagining Angel fainting or dying or, worse still, that gang coming to find him. '

Angel was there.'

'Angel?' Jude sat up so suddenly that the camp bed nearly tipped over.

'Sssh.' Poppy giggled nervously.

'I thought he'd gone away. We haven't seen him

for ages. How did he get in?'

'He broke a window. He was scared and needed somewhere to hide. He had a revolting cut on his arm which I had to bandage.'

'Broken glass, I suppose.'

'No. It was a stab wound.'

'A stab wound?' Jude gasped. 'Who was he hiding from? Why didn't he go to hospital?'

Jude jumped on to the bed and sat looking at Poppy. Poppy sat up too, so that they were face to face in the dim room. It was such a relief to tell the story, and it tumbled out in such a muddle that even Poppy scarcely understood what she was trying to explain.

Luckily Jude had a sharp mind. She summed up, 'So Angel's been stabbed but he can't go to hospital because he'll be in trouble with his dad and the police. And he's hiding out in your house because he's afraid he's hurt one of his mates and the rest of the gang will come after him. Is that right?'

'Quite right.' Poppy suddenly felt enormously sleepy. Jude might be annoying at times but she had plenty of determination.

'We'll go and see Angel first thing in the morning,' continued Jude. 'I'll tell Mum that your mum wants you to go to Mass to pray for your grandma and that I'm keeping you company. God won't mind, when it's such a good cause. Poppy, are you awake?'

'Yes,' said Poppy, as she fell asleep.

Chapter Four

It was so warm and bright when Poppy and Jude woke up (both in the same bed) that they had started putting on shorts before they remembered their going-to-church plan.

Jude's mum saw them off after a breakfast of chocolate muffins and crispy bacon. 'You are good girls,' she said.

'Well, we are good,' commented Jude as the door shut behind them, 'even if not how she thinks.' She pulled out something from her pocket. 'A muffin for Angel.'

'That's clever,' said Poppy. 'He must be starving.' She tried to walk confidently like Jude, who was a step or two ahead with her pony-tail swinging, but she couldn't help worrying about what they'd find. She half-wished Angel had gone off without waiting for her.

Both girls looked left and right as if they were crossing a road, before Poppy got out her door key.

'All clear,' announced Jude.

Poppy turned the key in the lock and pushed open the door gingerly.

Jude followed close behind her.

'Hello,' whispered Poppy, as if she was afraid of being overheard.

'It feels empty,' whispered Jude.

'Well, I didn't make him up.'

'Of course you didn't.'

Side by side, they pushed open the kitchen door. Despite the half-light because the curtains were still drawn, they could see there was nobody there. Poppy pulled Jude in and pointed to the floor. 'Look.'

'Blood!' Jude took a hasty step backwards.

They crossed the narrow corridor to the living room door.

'Hello.' Poppy spoke a little louder than before. 'Angel?'

This time there was a sound, more like a groan than a word.

'Perhaps the gang have come and got him,' hissed Jude, clutching at Poppy's arm. 'And now they're lying in wait for us!'

'Sshh.' Poppy had forgotten how Jude always liked to heighten the drama, even when things were quite dramatic enough. She shook her off and opened the door. It was even darker than the kitchen.

'Angel? Are you there?'

'I'm lying on the settee. You gone blind or something?'

The two girls stepped forward. Jude would have put on the light but Poppy stopped her. 'Are you all right?'

'Arm's throbbing like it's got a drum kit inside.' His voice suddenly changed. 'Who's that with you?'

'It's only Jude. She wants to help.'

'Hi, Angel.'

'So now the whole world knows where I am.'

'I suppose that's a compliment.'

Instead of answering, Angel groaned and turned over. 'I'm so hot, I'm sweating and my arm's like a furnace, a throbbing, beating furnace.'

'I'll open a window.' Jude darted across the room.

'Don't do that! Didn't Poppy tell you I'm in hiding?'

'Sorry.'

Poppy came and sat by Angel. She could feel waves of heat coming off him. 'I think you've got a fever. I'll get a thermometer from the bathroom, then we'll know for sure.'

When Poppy came back, Jude was putting her cardigan over Angel, who was protesting, 'I said I'm too hot, not too cold.'

'Fevers can give you a chill if you're not careful,' said Jude bossily, 'then you get pneumonia and die.'

'Cheers for that.'

Poppy quickly stuck the thermometer in his mouth before he could say anything more. The trouble was, when it gave a little ping and Poppy took it out, nobody could remember what it should read.

'Normal is thirty-eight,' said Jude firmly.

'I'm sure it's less than that,' worried Poppy. 'Or much more if it's Fahrenheit. It's all so muddling.'

Angel shut his eyes. 'I'm hot, that's all, man. And my arm hurts.'

'It says thirty-nine, I think.' Poppy peered at the thermometer in the semi-darkness. 'So whoever's right, he's miles above normal.'

'You two playing at doctors,' muttered Angel. 'Why don't you just leave me alone.'

'There's gratitude!' began Jude. She fumbled in her pocket. 'I even brought you a chocolate muffin.'

'Not hungry.'

Poppy interrupted them. 'Angel's right. What he needs is a real doctor.' She came close to where

Angel lay and tried to look determined.

'You know I can't.' Angel sounded defensive. 'I don't want to be in more trouble than I am already, do I.'

Sensing that he was less fierce about it than he had been the evening before, Poppy pressed on. 'What if we found a doctor who's a friend?'

'You know a doctor?'

'Will's mum,' said Poppy.

'Will's mum is definitely a GP,' agreed Jude. 'But would she tell?'

'We'll have to ring Will.'

Will was in Poppy and Jude's class at school. He had been an important part of the team that had nearly managed to spring Poppy's dad from prison. It might have worked, except that Big Frank had been sent to a prison at the top of a rocky island. But that was all before Poppy knew he was guilty.

'OK.' said Angel grudgingly. 'See what Will has to say.'

It was no surprise to Poppy and Jude when Will said he was coming round straight away. His mum gave him more freedom than theirs. Five minutes later he walked through the door, a small, slightly hunched figure but talking excitedly.

'Hi, Angel, Poppy, Jude. Was I *bored* before you called me! Have you ever read a book called *The Big Fun Album*? Well, don't.' Pushing his floppy hair back from his pale forehead and without drawing breath, he continued, 'Not much good with my mum, I'd say. Hospital much better.'

Angel gave a yelp of protest and then shut his eyes again, so Poppy began straight away to tell Will the whole story and why Angel was holed up in Poppy's house.

Will listened carefully. Having been ill so much, he was good at that. Then he sat on a chair with his legs up and looked knowing – rather like the caterpillar in *Alice in Wonderland*. 'Can't we have some light?'

'No!' grunted Angel.

'If your Flyers haven't found you yet, they won't now,' pointed out Poppy. Either Angel was convinced, or he was too weak to object any more, so Poppy went over and pulled back one of the curtains. The flood of sunlight immediately made the room more cheerful – at least, until Jude squealed, 'Look at the blood!'

'It's seeped through the bandage.' Angel bent over his arm with interest.

'But there's some on my cardigan. Mum will kill me!'

'I told you I was hot. Shouldn't have put it over me.'

'I was helping you!'

'Shut up, Jude.' Poppy put her hands over her ears and turned to Will imploringly. 'What do you think?'

'What I think is, we've got four problems.' As he spoke, Will ticked them off on his fingers: 'Number one, Angel's wound; number two, Angel's dad; number three, the police and number four, the boy Angel knocked down. What's he called, Angel?'

'Snake.'

'Lovely...' commented Jude.

'And what about Angel's mum?' suggested Poppy. 'She must be worried stiff.'

'I've stayed away before, haven't I,' muttered Angel. 'She didn't even notice. Ever since Eloise took over.'

'Who's Eloise?' asked Jude. 'Pretty name.'

'Not a pretty person. My mum's sitter. Big and bossy. Should be called Hippopotamus, for all her trampling.' Angel's face was so disgusted that first Jude and then Poppy giggled.

'You're sitting on my feet, Jude,' objected Angel, as she sat down on the couch.

'It's not your feet that've been stabbed, is it.'

'You think you're a nurse, then you sit on your patient.' Angel gave her a kick.

'Not so ill now.'

'What we need to do is this!' shouted Will suddenly, in a voice quite unlike his own. 'Action point one: I take Angel to my mum's surgery, tomorrow morning...'

'If he's still alive,' interrupted Jude.

'Action point two,' continued Will, glowering at Jude, 'Poppy and Jude go to wherever this gang of Angel's hangs out, to find out if this Snake is alive or dead.'

There was a thoughtful silence. Then Angel said, 'Would be good to know. Relieve my mind.'

'Are they dangerous?' Jude was sucking her finger.

'Not where you're concerned.' Angel looked at her pityingly. 'You can treat them like zoo animals. Just take a look and see if Snake is there.'

'How do we find them?' asked Poppy.

'Easy. Where do you think you find flyers? Under the flyover.'

'You can draw them a map,' said Will, gleaming with the satisfaction of his plans being taken seriously.

'How do we know which is Snake?' Poppy was

nervously pulling at strands of her hair so it stood out like a frizzy halo.

'Easy,' repeated Angel. 'He's over six feet. Dark skin and dyed white hair done in a Mohican.'

'You'll be hard put to recognise him, then,' said Will sarcastically.

'Lime green jacket. And "Snake" is written on the back. In red. Dripping like blood.'

'Oooh,' shivered Jude.

'Smokes, too. One roll-up after another. Lives for the gang. He'll either be there or dead.'

There was another pause before Jude whispered, 'Are you sure he won't attack us?'

'He's not interested in little girls like you. Now go. Gratitude and all that. But I need rest. Draw the curtains. My head's doing a tom-tom.'

Too shocked to disobey, Poppy and Jude left. Will called after them, 'I'll get a map out of Angel and drop it round later.'

The last they heard was a groan from Angel.

Chapter Five

Poppy looked up at the sky. The sun glinted sharply off the parked cars. She turned to Jude. 'Your mum will think we're very holy. We've been away ages.'

'I'll say it was a long sermon and we lit a candle afterwards for your grandma.' Jude skipped ahead of Poppy, before calling back, 'My dad's Italian, don't forget. In Italy we go to Mass with my grandma and it lasts for hours.'

Poppy ran to catch up, then slowed again. 'Odd, isn't it, seeing Angel so down?'

Jude stopped abruptly. 'If you had a hole in your arm, you wouldn't exactly be bouncing around.'

He was always so on top of things.' Poppy frowned thoughtfully. 'Like he knew more than we did.'

'He could hardly write when we first met him,' pointed out Jude.

'He still seemed cleverer than us,' insisted Poppy.

'And look where his cleverness got him!' exclaimed Jude, wagging her head..

'And us too,' Poppy said glumly.

'Going to see his gang, you mean.' Jude began to walk very fast. Her face looked rigid.

'I suppose we're going to spy on them.' Poppy jogged along at her side.

'They're only boys,' puffed Jude, who was now running. 'Like Rico and Ben.'

'I don't think your brothers would knife anybody!' yelled Poppy and, either because they had nothing more to say or because they were running too fast, neither said another word until they arrived home.

'Poppy! Where have you two been?' Jude's mum let them in and grabbed Poppy's arm. 'Your mother's rung twice. I'm not sure she believed me at first when I said you were in church. She was pleased, of course.' Sally led Poppy to the phone in the living room. 'Ring her mobile number. She says you know it. I'll leave you to speak to her.' Pushing Jude out of the room, she closed the door.

Poppy picked up the receiver. She didn't have a good feeling about this call.

'Poppy! Poppy! Oh! Oh!' Her mum was crying and talking at the same time.

'I can't hear you properly, Mum. Are you speaking Polish?'

'Your grandmama – she is dead.' Poppy heard that all right. 'In the night. At least she sleeps. But now your grandpapa. He cannot manage. I must stay. Long. Longer. Oh my beautiful Poppy, will you be happy with Jude's nice family?'

In the rush of her mum's words, Poppy felt her spirits sinking. Irena might be Polish and emotional, but they were a pair. With her dad away, they'd grown very close. However she knew there was only one answer to her mum's question.

'Fine. I'll be fine.'

Poppy and Jude were playing with a hosepipe in the garden after lunch when Will rang the door bell.

Sally showed him outside. 'It's your friend,' she said, adding cheerily, 'I'll bring some cake.'

'Hi,' said Poppy and Jude, pulling at their wet swimsuits. Will, fully dressed in long trousers, looked serious.

'I've got the thing I promised,' he said conspiratorially.

Poppy sighed, and Jude frowned. It had been such fun playing in the sunshine that they had managed to blot out the picture of Angel huddled up in the darkness, filled with pain and fear.

'Don't get me wet,' yelped Will, as Jude flicked the hosepipe.

'I'll turn it off,' she said reluctantly.

Will rubbed his sweating face. It was hot in the garden. 'Shall I show you here?'

'Oh, you mean the map,' said Jude airily, as if she hadn't known what he was there for all along.

'No, my pet canary,' replied Will crossly.

They sat on the edge of the big trampoline facing away from the house. Will extracted from his pocket a piece of paper folded into many squares. Poppy swatted a fly attracted by her wet hair and Jude tucked up her leg and pulled out a piece of grass from between her toes.

'You see here,' began Will, bending intently over the paper.

'I can't see, actually,' said Jude.

'Sorry.' Will leant back.

'I suppose that's the flyover,' Poppy pointed.

'No,' Will frowned, 'That's the bit that shows whether it's North, South, East or West. There's the flyover.' He put his finger on the spot.

Jude smiled sweetly. 'I thought that was

an aeroplane!'

'I've always heard that girls have no idea where they are, or anything else, either,' said Will through gritted teeth, 'but you two aren't even trying!' He raised his voice. 'Don't you want to help Angel?'

Poppy looked at Jude guiltily. Of course she wanted to help Angel – he was her friend – but on the other hand, the last thing she wanted was to go on a search for a dangerous gang in a part of London where they'd never been and their parents would never let them go.

'I suppose we'll have to go when it's dark,' said Poppy in a small voice. 'Otherwise they'd see us.'

'It doesn't get dark till eight,' said Jude. 'We'll never be allowed out on our own.'

'We'll have to think of something going on,' suggested Will.' Maybe I could have a party.'

Both Poppy and Jude looked at Will with surprise. He'd been ill for so much of his childhood that he'd never made any friends except them and still seemed a loner – very unpartyish.

'Not a real party,' Will added, seeing their doubtful look. 'A watching-a-movie party. Some evenings my mum leaves me alone.'

'I suppose it might work.' Poppy pushed back

her thick hair from her face and had another try at understanding the map.

'There's the flyover,' explained Will, 'and you know that road. It's next to the bus stop on the way to the prison. Do you remember when we tried to get your dad out of there?' he added, eyes gleaming.

'It may bring back happy memories for you,' replied Poppy crossly, 'but he's still in prison and it doesn't make me bounce with joy.'

'I thought he liked his island prison,' said Jude, 'although I thought it was horrible. He was singing in *Guys and Dolls* when we went to see him.'

Poppy frowned furiously. 'He doesn't like it.'

'He should never have gone to prison,' said Will, which wasn't quite true, but at least he meant well.

An awkward silence fell, before he began again to explain the way to the flyover.

Bit by bit, Poppy and Jude got the hang of it. 'It would take about twenty minutes walking and I could come part of the way.'

'Why can't you come all the way!' Jude jumped off the trampoline and stood in front of him. 'You're afraid, aren't you?'

'No, I'm not!' Will went bright red in the face.

'It's the thought of that tall dyed Mohican boy. I know.'

Will went even redder. 'Didn't you hear what Angel said? Girls don't count with them. They won't even notice you.'

'Thanks!' said Jude, flouncing. 'Are you saying that you,' she stopped and stared at him scornfully, 'would get more attention than me and Poppy?'

'Sshh, Jude.' Poppy could see tears in Will's eyes. 'You don't have to be nasty. If you really want to know, I'm scared, and I know you are too.'

Before Jude could answer, her mum called loudly, 'Tea's up!'

They sat in silence for a while, but Poppy could see that Will still had something he wanted to say. Judging by his nervous expression, it wasn't anything cheerful.

Poppy turned to him. 'What is it, Will?'

Will gulped. 'My mum's out tonight.' The girls looked so shocked that he added, 'The sooner, the better, from Angel's point of view.'

It was surprisingly easy to get permission to watch

a film at Will's house. Jude's mum and dad were going out anyway, so Rico would be in charge. He said he would pick them up at eight-thirty.

'Isn't that a bit early?' asked Poppy, when they were getting ready. Will had already gone home.

'Oh, I'll ring Rico,' said Jude cheerfully, 'and put him off a bit. But we might be back before eight-thirty.'

'I hope so,' said Poppy fervently. 'What do you think about this grey sweat shirt?'

Jude looked at her consideringly. They had agreed they should look as inconspicuous as possible. 'The trouble is, your hair's so bright and there's so much of it. Why don't you wear a hat?'

'I'd die of heat. I'll try and tie it back.' Poppy thought Jude had rather overdone the spy bit. She was dressed in black from head to foot, including gloves she'd pinched from her mum. 'You don't think you'll call attention to yourself dressed like that?' she asked tentatively.

'Perhaps I'll leave off the gloves,' conceded Jude, who was beginning to look rather hot herself.

It was still light when they walked over to Will's

house, escorted by Rico. On the way they passed Poppy's front door. Rico turned to look.

'That's where you live, isn't it? Anything you need?'

'No, no.' Poppy hurried on, but not before she'd clocked the still-drawn curtains and felt a silence that made her shiver. She wished Rico could come with them on their mission. Then she remembered Angel had told them that big boys were more at risk than what he called 'little girls'.

On Will's doorstep, Jude said a firm goodbye to her brother so he wouldn't come inside and see that Will was alone. 'Nine o'clock's better than eight-thirty. Tomorrow's the last day of the holidays. We can have a lie-in.'

'Bossy, bossy,' said Rico good-humouredly before striding off. Poppy looked after him longingly.

Inside the house, Will was rushing about in a wired-up way. 'I can't find the map!' he wailed.

'I've got it.' Poppy waved it in his face.

'It's still light,' Jude peered out of the window.

'We should watch some of the film, anyway,' said Poppy. 'Your mums are sure to ask about it.'

Afterwards, none of them could remember a single thing about the film. They were far too nervous to concentrate. Most of the time they were jumping up and down to see how dark it was getting.

At last – 'Let's go!' – Will led them to the door. He waved his arm heroically. 'Into the lions' den!'

'I've always preferred tigers,' said Jude.

'Give me cats,' said Poppy, and laughing, they exited the house with a series of high fives, before running in a bunch up the road.

Chapter Six

They soon slowed down. They were nervous, and somehow even the streets they knew well look strange. Through the open door of the corner shop where Poppy always stopped to wave at Rita at the till, there was a big unknown man. Two chairs had been brought outside, where old men sat smoking. At the café further along where Poppy sometimes had a quiet cup of hot chocolate with her mum, there was now a crowd of noisy young men and women drinking cans of beer. By the entrance to the small supermarket, there was a figure bundled up in a sleeping bag and scarves begging from passers-by. Although it was a sad sight, this evening even he seemed threatening.

'It's getting dark now,' said Poppy. She was thinking that her poor mum would have a fit if she knew what they were up to.

'Check,' said Will in his leader-of-the-mission voice.

Jude said nothing, and Poppy thought her face looked as pale as a ghost's in the waning light.

They had passed through the area they knew and entered streets where the street lamps threw shadows instead of light, and plastic bags of half-eaten chicken bones or sticky bottles lay in the gutters or by the doors. Then they were crossing through an estate of high-rises, two of the tallest coated in scaffolding and apparently empty. The third had a scattering of broken windows in a towering wall of stained cement. Where they walked, an attempt had been made at a garden but all that remained were a few small trees broken off at waist height and some scruffy shrubs more grey than green. A dry wind blew newspapers and other rubbish around the blistered tarmac.

Jude jumped, as an empty can rolled to her feet. 'I don't like it here,' she said. 'Can't we go another way?'

Will looked at the map, but it was almost too dark to see. Half the lights on the estate weren't working. 'I think this is where Angel lives.' He attempted a smile. 'I suppose he's used to it.'

'I expect it's nicer inside,' said Poppy hopefully. 'His mum and his sister and brother always looked very smart.'

'If his dad's such a gangster,' said Jude, 'you'd think he'd do better for himself.'

'He mostly seems to be in prison,' pointed out Poppy.

Up to now the place had been remarkably empty of people but suddenly, as if entering a stage, several groups came from different directions.

'Let's move!' said Jude nervously.

'They're just ordinary people,' said Poppy, telling herself that it was only the uncared-for gloom of the estate which made everything seem threatening.

'Why are we standing here anyway?' asked Jude.

Will was peering at the map again. 'I guess we go left, round the side of that building.'

'What do you mean, you guess?' Jude sounded extremely suspicious.

'It wasn't easy to make a map,' said Will defensively. 'Angel couldn't use his right hand, as you know, so he tried to draw with his left. But that didn't work, so he told me to do it, but he wasn't very clear because he was in pain and...'

'You mean, we're lost!' interrupted Jude. 'I thought boys were supposed to have a much better sense of direction than girls.' She seemed pleased to have caught Will out.

Poppy thought how silly they were to argue. A family had just passed by, and she noted that they weren't in hoodies and the little girl with them looked rather like someone in their school. 'Let's try going left,' she said firmly, and because she set out at once, Will and Jude stopped trying to score off each other and followed her.

The wind blew fiercely as they skirted the base of one of the scaffolded buildings and Poppy felt her hair standing on end, as if she was scared. But actually, she was more excited than scared. This was a real adventure and Angel really needed help.

They reached the other side of the estate.

'Angel told me we'd see the motorway from here,' said Will.

But they heard it first: that continuous low roar that surrounds big cities all over the world. 'It sounds like a giant animal,' whispered Poppy. She moved closer to Jude and Will. The strange sound was far scarier than people or rattling cans.

'It's just traffic.' Will seemed to have recovered his confidence. 'Cars, lorries, vans, motorbikes.'

'We know what traffic is,' said Jude.

Poppy pulled herself together. How silly to be frightened of a noise. 'Where do we go now?'

'Right up to it and underneath, Angel said.' Will put the map back in his pocket. 'He said there're all kind of things under it – football grounds, riding schools.'

'Riding schools – as in horses?' asked Poppy wonderingly.

'Doesn't sound likely,' puffed Jude. They were walking quite fast now and the din above them was getting louder with every step. Poppy could see that they were heading for the point where two black strips of motorway passed each other overhead. The cars were completely invisible, however, which made the great moving noise even odder.

'I'm only telling you what Angel said.' Will stopped for a moment, and Poppy remembered he was not supposed to be too energetic. 'I expect he knows the area better than you.'

'Horses hate loud noise, that's all.'

'If you'd seen the film or read the book, *War Horse*, you'd know that horses fought in the First World War with shell fire all around them.'

'Horses can't fight...' began Jude.

'Please don't start arguing again, you two,' interrupted Poppy.

So they walked on silently, and where there

weren't lights, the sky was completely black and the motorways tore across it making huge cavernous roofs for whatever lay beneath.

Poppy looked over to the right. 'There are lights under there.'

They stopped again. Behind them was a little row of houses that seemed to be made of hardboard and corrugated iron.

'What a place to live!' Jude shouted, and lowered her voice. 'Funny, it doesn't seem so noisy now we're close.'

'Someone's been having a clear-out.' Poppy pointed to a sofa, a lamp, and other bits of broken, dirty furniture.

'I think someone's living there,' said Jude. 'There's a sleeping bag.'

Poppy shivered. 'I suppose they can go under the motorway if it rains.'

Meanwhile, Will was craning his head upwards. 'Angel told me to look for a tall electronic advertising hoarding that starts in the ground and goes up through the gap in the two motorways, so that drivers can see it as they pass by. But I can't see a thing.'

Both girls looked up but neither could see anything either.

'What's it advertising?' asked Jude.

'Why are we looking for it?' asked Poppy.

'The gang meets at the bottom of it,' answered Will simply. 'And of course I don't know what they're advertising. Might be baby food, for all I know. Anyway, Angel said to just go on in if we can't see it.'

So they went on in and it got darker and even stranger, because every wall and each of the gigantic pillars that supported the motorway were painted with amazing graffiti in swirling colours of orange, purple, pink, lime green, scarlet – flowers, faces, gigantic butterflies, snails, lizards, snakes and dragons.

'Wow!' exclaimed Poppy, 'They're beautiful!' But they were also frightening: too big, too bright in the darkness, plus there was the vibration of the traffic rumbling over their heads. Amongst the graffiti were padlocked doors, blue and red and yellow, leading to what seemed to be clubs or even shops.

'I suppose they're closed because it's Sunday,' whispered Jude.

At that moment, six boys on skateboards appeared from behind a pillar heading straight towards them. At the very last minute, with loud whoops and catcalls they swung round and headed off into the blackness.

'Was that Angel's gang?' asked Poppy, when she'd recovered from the surprise.

'If it was, then Will shouldn't be with us, according to Angel,' said Jude. 'But I'd rather he stayed.'

Poppy looked at Will. 'They came and went so quickly, I couldn't see what any of them looked like. But I think you should stay too. Angel's not right about everything. Otherwise he wouldn't have got himself stabbed.'

Will smiled. 'I'm hardly your macho bodyguard. More like "wimpy Will".'

'We called you that before we knew you,' said Jude.

'We've known you're very brave for ages,' added Poppy. 'Ever since we tried to get my dad out of prison. Even if we didn't manage it.'

Will looked pleased that Poppy had forgiven him for his earlier comment about her dad and, taking the role of commander once more, led them forward to where Poppy had seen the lights.

'I smell something funny.' Jude sniffed theatrically.

'Horses,' joked Poppy.

'Not so funny,' said Will. For there ahead of them

was a fenced ring in which horses were circling under glaring spotlights. 'Didn't I tell you!'

Poppy and Jude stared, hardly able to believe their eyes.

'There's the football ground!' exclaimed Will. And there it was, also brightly lit and, judging by the shouts, a highly competitive game was in progress.

'It's like a whole other world under here,' said Poppy.

Will had got out the map again. He looked down, frowned, looked up, then down again.

'Well?' said Jude. 'Shall I book us in for a ride?'

Will ignored her. 'I think we go between the riding and the football.' He peered upwards as he had earlier. 'If only we could see the advertising tower. It must be somewhere.'

Poppy and Jude weren't so sure, but they followed Will.

Once they'd passed the two sports grounds, they entered a kind of garden – at least, there were some biggish bushes and a couple of seats made out of bricks – but it was so dimly lit that they could see very little. It seemed to be entirely empty and, now they'd got used to the continuous rumble overhead and they couldn't hear the footballers any longer, very very quiet.

'It's spooky,' whispered Jude.

Poppy was imagining figures jumping out from behind the bushes, but it seemed better not to say so out loud.

They crossed the garden towards a row of columns supporting one of the motorways. Each column had a vast question mark painted in dripping red. Like blood, thought Poppy, but didn't say that either. This was the point where the motorways crossed, so that there was space of sky on either side, shaped like two crescents, above their heads.

'Found it!'

Jude and Will jumped as Poppy let out a loud shriek. 'Up there! Look! A huge man with glowing orange muscles and a silly face.'

'It's the advert.' Will grabbed Poppy's arm. 'Now we've just got to trace it down to ground level.'

'Over here,' called Poppy, who was already running off. Then she stopped so abruptly that both Will and Jude ran into her. 'I think that's the place.'

Ahead, but half-hidden by one of the pillars and set back in its own space, was a tiled tower surrounded by a steep mesh fence with gates and a padlock, except that the padlock was broken and the gates were open.

They approached cautiously. 'There doesn't seem to be anyone there,' whispered Will.

Poppy studied the graffiti on the tower. It was black, yellow and red and included several giant fists and outsized eyes. She looked down at the floor, covered with broken bits of wood, empty cans, jagged glass and a couple of what looked like old drainpipes. Between them, sprouts of grass straggled up. Her eyes fixed on something just beyond the entrance. She felt herself go pale and her legs began to shake.

'Someone is there. There's a cigarette stub. And it's still burning.' Without thinking, she went closer.

'Poppy!' warned Jude, who was some way behind her. 'Come back!'

'Poppy!' called Will, who was hanging back beside Jude.

'Poppy!' mimicked a horribly grating voice, and from behind one of the painted eyes on the tower stepped a tall, unmistakable figure.

'Run, Poppy!' screamed Jude and Will.

Chapter Seven

Perhaps Poppy would have run, if she hadn't been staring so hard to move. This had to be Snake, the man they'd come to find, all six foot plus of him, complete with dyed white Mohican hair and a lime-green jacket.

In two long strides he was at her side. Then it was too late to run.

'Gotchya!' He grabbed Poppy triumphantly, calling over his shoulders, 'Hey, bros. See what's rolled in.'

From behind the tower emerged three men – more boys than men, Poppy tried to tell herself. They were a foot shorter than Snake.

'Let me go!' she shouted.

But Snake only laughed and dragged her through the steel mesh gate. 'Want to have a look, do you? Look till your eyes pop out.' He shook her so hard that her teeth rattled and she thought her eyes really might pop out.

'Who's she?' asked one boy.

'Two more behind,' said another.

'Give Snake a smoke. Calm him down,' suggested the third.

'Don't like strangers on my turf,' growled Snake, but he accepted a cigarette and let Poppy go.

'You hurt me,' said Poppy, rubbing her arm. After her first fright, she was feeling braver. 'I was only walking by.'

'So why've your mates run?' asked boy number one, who had a strong lisp.

'They didn't want to be snatched, did they.' Poppy stared at him defiantly.

'You shouldn't be here,' said boy number two.

Poppy considered replying, 'It's a free world,' before thinking better of it. Her arm was still sore.

'Why are you snooping around?' asked boy number three, which was a slightly different question and reminded Poppy of why she was there. Snake was alive! She had discovered Snake was alive, so now all she had to do was get away and tell Angel. However, something told her that if she made a dash for it, Snake would reach out a long arm.

'I was curious,' she said, trying to sound sweet

and a bit simple. 'I wanted to know what was under here.'

'So now you know.' Snake stamped out his cigarette under his boot. 'Bring her round the back.'

He's just an overgrown bully, Poppy told herself, as the three boys took her on either side and marched her nearer the tower. But her heart was beating painfully hard and her legs had started trembling again. After all, Angel had been stabbed. Maybe she should kick out and try to run.

The other side of the tower had been turned into a den with sleeping bags, boxes to sit on, even an old cupboard with a couple of cans on top. Poppy realised she absolutely didn't want to go there and was gearing herself up for a breakaway, when a voice began shouting loudly.

Snake and his friends swung round. Poppy couldn't make out what the voice was saying but the boys seemed to know well enough. One of them picked up a brick and the others a stick and a plank. Led by Snake they headed out, yelling war-like challenges.

From being the centre of attention, Poppy was now forgotten. Cautiously she edged out behind them.

Coming towards them was a gang – at least seven

or eight of them. Mostly they were bigger, too, with black shiny jackets, gelled-up hair and pale jeans – almost a uniform. Poppy couldn't pretend to be sorry for Snake and his team but she certainly didn't want to be in their shoes – boots, that is. The sooner she did a runner, the better.

Then the leader of the advancing gang stopped and pointed directly at her. 'Who's she?' he bellowed, as if personally affronted by her presence.

Not for the first time, Poppy blamed her red hair for making her easily visible. The trouble was, that it had come out of its band and she could feel it standing up in its usual wild way.

'Nobody!' growled Snake. Which was hardly flattering but perhaps the best line. Poppy thought of adding, 'I really am nobody, honest,' and only just stopped herself giggling hysterically. Why couldn't they just get on and fight if they wanted to, and leave her out of it? Boys were so stupid.

Head high, she walked straight out of the gate, turned left and started back the way she'd first come – luckily, in the opposite direction from the two gangs. She decided that they'd have to knock her unconscious and pick her up bodily, if they wanted to stop her.

Not daring to look back, she heard shouted taunts and then the sound of something being thrown, and a yelp of pain. Nobody came after her so she walked more quickly, still not running because she'd heard dogs and other belligerent beasts always chased a running figure.

Now she was on the edge of the garden with the dusty bushes. Behind her the shouts were angrier and suddenly there were pounding feet. She still didn't turn her head but she knew they were coming her way.

'Here! In here!' The urgent voice seemed to be coming from one of the biggest shrubs. Poppy hesitated.

'It's Jude. We're hiding.'

'Quick!'

Poppy didn't hesitate, but dived blindly into the dark and prickly bush. In the middle was a hollow space, and huddled there were Jude and Will.

'Are we safe here?' Poppy whispered, her heart still racing.

'We can see out.' Will pushed aside a few branches, giving a clear view of the tower and the gangs.

'I thought they were coming after me.'

'Snake and his lot were running away from

the others. Look. They've got behind the fence and locked the gate.'

Now she was calmer, she could see quite clearly what was going on. 'That new lot are throwing things over.'

'Isn't that one of them trying to climb over, too?' Jude peered past Poppy. 'He's got a friend giving him a jump-up.'

'I'll tell you what,' Poppy sat back on her heels. 'I don't care what they do to each other, I just want to go home.' As she spoke, she remembered that she didn't have a home, not her own home, anyway. That made her think of Angel. 'We need to tell Angel about Snake as soon as possible.'

Jude looked at her watch but she couldn't see the time in the darkness.

'We should run, while they're busy trying to attack each other,' agreed Will.

'Let's creep out,' suggested Jude nervously.

'We can crawl from bush to bush,' said Will.

'Isn't that a bit much?,' Poppy said scornfully. After all, she was the one who'd done the escaping. 'I'm walking.'

'Walk, then. Slowly. Quietly. One at a time,' said Will, trying, Poppy thought, to establish his

leadership again.

So they walked out one at a time, threading their way from bush to bush. They were nearly at the end of the garden and in sight of the riding school where the lights were still bright, when they heard ugly shouts behind them.

Poppy looked round. She felt her stomach lurch with fear. The second gang, having failed to get over the railings, were racing towards them.

'Get into the riding school!' yelled Will.' They'll never come there.'

Running so hard her breath hurt, Poppy managed to tumble over a wooden fence into the area where a group of horses were parading sedately round. Unfortunately, both she and Jude hit the sawdust at the exact spot where a shaggy brown pony was passing by. While they lay helplessly, the pony neighed, bucked and shot off, leaving its rider on the ground.

'Where've you come from?' the rider, a girl not much older than them, demanded crossly.

Before Poppy or Jude could answer, a stout woman in jodhpurs came running over.

'Get out of my class!' she screeched even before she'd reached them. 'I'm ringing the police!'

'We can get out now,' said Will in a low voice from somewhere nearby, 'They've gone.'

'What are you doing just lying there, Jocasta?' The screech was nearly upon them. 'Go and catch Chocolate Drop this instant!'

'Sorry, Miss Hetherington-Pip,' said the fallen rider, getting up obediently and heading after the pony.

'I'm glad I'm not learning riding here,' muttered Poppy, as she headed back towards the wooden fence.

'Quite put me off,' agreed Jude, who was close behind.

'Still, Miss Hellishly Pip probably scared off the gang,' said Will, as they gathered together outside the riding school.

Poppy looked up and down. No sign of anything threatening. 'I think they heard her screaming "Police".'

At that moment the quiet was broken by the caterwauling of police sirens.

'How on earth did they get here so quickly?' exclaimed Jude.

'They can't actually get their cars in here,' said Will.

'They seem awfully close,' said Poppy nervously. 'They must have been lying in wait.'

The strange thing was that they felt guilty, although the worst thing they'd done was cause a rider to fall off her pony. She hadn't even been hurt.

'Let's go,' said Will. The cars had stopped now, although the sirens were still wailing.

'It wouldn't look good if the police picked us up and took us home,' said Jude in a very small voice. 'Can you imagine – with those sirens.'

They began to walk faster. They might not have done anything very bad, but their parents might think that being out at night on their own was very bad indeed. Only, Poppy thought sadly, her mum and dad were far away and would never know. Then she thought that Jude's mum might blame her for leading her daughter astray.

'What's that?' Will called. He had fallen behind with that pale-faced, tired look that reminded the girls he had a bad heart.

They all listened and, above the sound of their own hurrying footsteps, were others louder, faster and coming closer.

In a few moments the second gang, totally ignoring them, came racing by. A moment later the Flyers, led by Snake, whizzed past them. Another moment and four burly policemen, their radios buzzing with voices, came lumbering past. They didn't even glance at Poppy, Jude or Will.

'Phew!' exclaimed Will. They stopped and looked at each other. Then Poppy began to giggle.

'It was like the chase scene out of some old movie.'

Jude and Will began to laugh too. 'One good thing – no one's after us any more.'

'What about Miss Hideously Pip? She'll be after us with her riding whip.'

They were laughing too much to walk very fast so they were still under the motorway when the police reappeared in the distance ambling along, one talking into his radio mike.

'Pity,' commented Will. 'Obviously, they didn't catch anyone.'

'Let's make sure they don't catch us,' suggested Poppy, turning sharp right. 'We can get out this way.'

Chapter Eight

Escape from the dangerous world under the flyover made Poppy and Jude and Will go a little crazy.

They imitated Snake, shouting in threatening bass tones, 'Till your eyes pop out! Pop! Pop! Pop!' Then they became Miss 'Hit-her-over the head-Pip' in high falsetto. 'Pip! Pip! I'm coming to get you-u-u with my HORSE-WHI-I-I-P!' They dashed through the streets and this time they passed the estate and its grimly unkempt high-rises without a hint of fear.

They felt brave and successful. Mission accomplished. They knew Snake was alive (although they didn't think he deserved to be.) They only sobered up when they reached their own streets and everything was familiar again.

'What time is it?' asked Jude. Both she and Poppy had decided to leave their watches behind. So, it turned out, had Will.

'It feels very, very late.' Poppy peered at the sky. 'Isn't that the moon?'

'The moon doesn't move,' objected Will. 'That's an aeroplane.'

'No time to drop in on Angel, anyway,' said Jude.

'We could write him a note,' suggested Poppy, who wanted Angel to know the good news about Snake as soon as possible.

'If we had a pen,' said Will.

'Which we don't,' said Jude in a tight edgy voice. She began to walk quickly, almost running.

Poppy supposed Jude was worried about her mum finding out where they'd been. She was worried too; about Angel first, then about her mum in Poland, about her grandmama who'd died (even if she'd scarcely known her) and about her dad, Big Frank, stuck away in prison. Jude had no real worries. But Poppy could see even from her back that she'd gone into cross mode and, as usual, would be looking for someone to blame.

They were all relieved to reach Will's house. It was dark so – hooray! –at least his mum wasn't back. As he rushed around putting on lights, drawing curtains and turning on the TV, Poppy, feeling rather dazed, stood in the hallway and just watched.

She was going to join the others when she noticed a piece of paper on the floor. Bending, she picked it up. Scrawled across it were four words: CAN'T WAIT ANY MORE. Oh, no! Obviously Rico had already come to collect them.

'Jude!'

Jude came over, frowning. 'What is it now?'

'Rico's left a note. He must have been here earlier. Look!'

Jude took the note. She looked puzzled. 'Why do you think that's Rico's writing? He's not illiterate, you know.'

At that moment the door bell rang. 'Hello. Anyone at home?' It was Rico's deep male voice.

Pushing past Poppy, Jude opened the door and more or less flung herself at her brother. 'The film finished ages ago!'

What a liar, thought Poppy, stuffing the note in her pocket.

'You said you wanted extra time.' Rico smiled at Poppy and Will who'd appeared from the living room. 'Hi. Enjoy the movie?'

'Hmm. Erhm,' they muttered, not being good liars like Jude.

Stuffing the note in her pocket, Poppy followed Jude out.

'We'll talk tomorrow,' said Will, watching them go.

'Sure.' Jude gave him an off-hand wave.

They were halfway back to Jude's house before it struck Poppy that the note in her pocket really belonged to Will. It had come through his letter box on to his door mat. Lingering behind the others, she took it out and flattened it. Even under the street lamps she could tell exactly who had sent it. Someone who wasn't too good at writing and probably was using his left hand. In other words, Angel.

He must have left her house, dropped this note and gone who knows where. Remembering how bad his arm had been, it was hard to imagine what he was up to. And Will had promised to take him to see his GP mum the next morning.

Perhaps he was scared. Or delirious. Or he'd just gone home. Poppy hoped it was the last option. But then, why couldn't he write GONE HOME? It didn't make sense: CAN'T WAIT ANY MORE. They'd never said they were going round to see him tonight. A thought struck her: perhaps he'd been kidnapped and forced to write the note!

Poppy was now so far behind Jude and her brother that he shouted out, 'Come on, slowcoach, or we'll arrive on the doorstep at the same time as my mum and dad.'

Thinking how nice it must be to have a brother looking out for you, Poppy ran to catch them up.

Unfortunately, Jude was still in her edgy mood. 'I'll have a shower first,' she announced as soon as they'd stepped through the door.

'Fine,' agreed Poppy, following her upstairs.

'I'll bring you up a snack,' offered Rico, who was clearly some kind of saint. But then, the whole house was very foodie. Poppy thought nostalgically of her mum's Polish specialities: beetroot and yoghurt soup, potato dumplings or, on her birthday, poppy-seed cake. At the time she'd often complained and demanded burgers and chips instead. It was hard to believe that her mum had only left for Poland yesterday. So much had happened since.

'See you,' said Jude, collecting her night things and going into the bathroom where she bolted the door with an aggressive click.

Poppy wandered into Ben's room. Jude obviously wanted to be alone, so it would be better to sleep here tonight. She sat on the bed, then slowly began to undress.

After a while she heard Jude come out of the bathroom and go into her own room. The problem was, she really needed someone to talk to about

Angel. She crept along to the bathroom. Jude's door was shut.

Why did Jude have to be so changeable? She'd been keen on helping Angel. Maybe it was Post Traumatic Stress Syndrome. They had all been frightened under the motorway but it was she, Poppy, who'd been grabbed. Jude had run away. Poppy began to feel angry. But still, she needed someone to talk to.

As she got into her bed with its cold, unwelcoming bedclothes, she heard Jude's parents come in.

'Goodnight, Jude and Poppy!' they called from downstairs. 'If you're still awake, you shouldn't be!'

Poppy tried to obey. If only her head would stop whirling with images: Angel bleeding under the table, Snake grabbing hold of her, the other gang pounding towards her. How could she sleep after all that?

Right! She grabbed the note from under her pillow and ran straight into Jude's room. A street lamp outside gave enough light for her to see a hump in the bed. It hadn't stirred.

'Jude!'

No answer.

'Jude, I've got to talk to you.' Still no answer. Poppy went over and prodded her.' Wake up! I'm not going away.'

Jude turned over slowly and Poppy saw she really had been asleep. What a traitor!

'Hmm. What?' she mumbled.

'I've got something important to show you.'

'I'm so, so tired.' At last Jude pulled herself up and put on the bedside light. 'Oh, it's you.'

'Jude, this is serious. Angel left a note. He's run away.'

A ferocious expression sharpened Jude's blurry face and she stuffed her fingers into her ears. 'I don't want to hear that boy's name,' she hissed. 'I can't think why he's called Angel. He's dangerous. We could have been murdered out there. And all because of him. Just leave me out of it.' She turned over and curled into an unreceptive ball.

'But nothing bad happened to you!'

'Go away!'

'I won't. Angel's my friend. I thought he was yours.'

'Well, he's not. Not any more.' Suddenly, Jude sat up facing Poppy. 'And tomorrow I'm going to tell mum where we were tonight and she'll be horrified and blame you. In fact, she'll probably throw you out of the house. You're only here out of the kindness of our hearts, you know. We don't have to look after you and your bad boyfriend. It's disturbing our lives. So go away! Get out! And let me go to sleep!'

She slammed her head back down on the pillow, before getting up again to turn off the light.

Poppy was left shocked and trembling. She edged out of the room and crawled back into her cold bed. Her eyes bulged with tears but she blinked them back.

She knew she would lie awake all night. But the long day and the even longer evening, all the running and the hiding, had made her more exhausted than she realised. In a few minutes she was fast asleep.

Chapter Nine

White morning light came through Poppy's windows. She'd forgotten to draw the curtains the night before. In her dreams she heard scratching and pictured a large dog, perhaps a creamy Labrador.

'Poppy! It's me. Can I come in?'

Poppy rolled over and opened her eyes. Jude stood at the door. Immediately all the horrible things she'd said the night before flooded into Poppy's head. She couldn't think what to say, so she kept quiet.

'I'm sorry.' Jude came and sat on the end of Poppy's bed. 'But you shouldn't have woken me.'

Blaming me as usual, thought Poppy. 'Are you still going to tell your mum about last night?'

Jude collected her hair and tied it back with a band she took off her wrist. She seemed to be considering, and Poppy didn't like the calculating look on her face.

'Are you?'

'That depends,' said Jude. 'I really want you to stay here, incidentally.'

Poppy thought that it wasn't very incidental to her. She guessed there was a 'but' on the way.

'...But I won't have anything more to do with Angel and I don't think you should either, at least while you're living here.' Jude stared at Poppy, her dark brown eyes challenging her.

Poppy turned her head away. She knew she could never abandon Angel. She also knew she was a bad liar. Thinking hard, she decided Jude had no right to tell her how to lead her life, even if she was staying with her. 'So you won't tell your mum, and you won't see Angel?' she said.

'Right.' Jude looked relieved, as if Poppy had agreed with her terms.

'Fine,' continued Poppy, doing her best to smile. 'So let's enjoy our final day of freedom before school begins.'

Funnily enough, they did. Sally, Jude's mum, had planned to take them shopping for last-minute school things and then to the swimming pool.

Before they left, Poppy wrote a note to Will: *Angel's gone. We've got to find him. Ring my mobile after*

after lunch. Poppy knew Jude would be out then, visiting her aunt. She put the note, with Angel's, in an envelope and when they passed Will's house slipped it through the letter box while Jude chattered to her mother.

At least *she* hadn't deserted Angel.

The only weird moment came as they were heading back for lunch.

'Do you want to see if there're any letters for you at your home?' Sally asked suddenly.

Poppy and Jude looked at each other in alarm. What if Jude's mum went in and saw the blood and signs of someone having been there? She'd probably phone the police.

'Your mother gave me the key,' continued Sally gaily, and she pulled it out of her bag.

'I'll go in,' said Poppy quickly.

'Oh, all right.' Jude's mum handed over the key and both girls sighed with relief.

Even so, Poppy's heart beat too fast. What would she find there? Her home had become a place where she hardly dared go.

But everything was quiet. She picked up a few letters lying on the mat and hurriedly, in case Jude's mum decided to follow her after all, peered first into the kitchen, then the living room. Nothing had changed. The drawn curtains, the spots of blood, the rumpled sofa.

And no Angel.

She ran back out.

'Anything interesting?' Jude indicated the letters with assumed casualness.

'Nothing.' Poppy stuffed them in with her shopping. It wasn't Jude's business any more.

In fact, she'd spotted a letter from her dad. He didn't write often and usually her mum grabbed the letter. Once she'd read it, sometimes she would pass it over to Poppy with a sigh and a shake of her head. 'Oh, your papa,' she would say. 'How we love him! How we miss him!'

Lately, Poppy had tried to imagine what it would be like when Big Frank came back. In the last year he'd been away, they'd only visited him twice – he said it upset him too much, and it was a long journey to the island where he was held – so she pictured him as he'd been before he went into prison. He'd been the biggest, loudest, funniest man in the world, never serious when he could make a joke. All her friends thought she was lucky to have him as her dad:

He'd been not just her dad, but her hero, Big Frank. Then he went to prison and she had to think about him differently. In one way it was a relief when he didn't want to see her. But of course, he wouldn't be in prison for ever.

If she was honest, she couldn't quite see him fitting back into her life with her mum. Their days were so orderly, with her mum's piano pupils going in and out, and her school-work. At least, they had been, until Irena went to Poland and Angel turned up.

Poppy fingered the envelope in her pocket. If her dad had been there, he might have known how to deal with Angel. There was no point in sending on the letter to Poland. She would open it as soon as she had time on her own.

'What are you looking so po-faced about?' Jude called from the steps outside.

'Nothing.' Poppy hurried to join her.

After lunch, when everybody else had gone out, Poppy sat in the garden on the swing. She put the letter and her mobile beside her. It was such a relief to be by herself that she did nothing for a bit.

The sun was bright in her eyes so she pulled down the shade, then pushed with her legs so that she swung gently. Everything went misty and quiet.

She was woken from her doze by her mobile playing the Star Trek theme.'Hi.'

'It's me, Will. Where's Angel gone? What did he mean? He doesn't even know yet that Snake's fine – so fine that he grabbed you and got into a fight.'

'Slow down, Will.' Poppy knew she had to concentrate but still felt misty.

'I can't. At least, I can. I have. I was running a temperature last night so my mum's keeping me in bed. I hate being ill.'

Poppy's heart sank. No Jude, because she didn't want to be involved, and no Will because he was ill. 'I'm sorry.'

'But what are we going to do about Angel? His arm was terrible and he had a much higher temperature than me.'

'It's not we,' said Poppy gloomily. 'It's me. Jude won't have anything more to do with him. She says he's dangerous.'

'True.'

'And she might tell her mum about last night.'

'Traitor!' exclaimed Will.

They were both silent for a minute. Poppy heard a bird singing overhead and wished she could just switch off and enjoy it.

'I'm hoping he's gone home,' she said. 'That would be the sensible thing to do.'

'Sensible? Angel, sensible?'

'No,' agreed Poppy. 'It might be worth checking it out, though. If I knew where he lived. I like his mum, and his dad tried to help us get my dad out of prison.'

'There is one thing I was going to tell you.' Poppy heard Will move further away from the phone, then the crackle of paper. 'I looked at the map Angel made with me and I've just seen a cross near one of the tower blocks and a squiggle that looks as if it says "My place". It's not very clear. If you went over there, you could find out for sure whether he's gone home.'

Poppy felt both hopeful and full of dread. She took a deep breath. 'I could go there now. Quickly, before Jude and her mum get back.'

'And pick up the map before my mum's back. She's at afternoon surgery.'

'I'm on my way.' Poppy leapt up, and only then noticed the unopened envelope from her dad.

It was hard to miss it, with Her Majesty's Prison Castlerock stamped all over it. Once again, she stuffed the letter into her pocket.

Chapter Ten

Angel stuffed a couple of paracetamols in his mouth. He'd taken a packet from Poppy's bathroom when he'd climbed out of the window the evening before. They made him feel strange, as if everything was happening to someone else, but they also made the pain in his arm and his head bearable. He'd seen his mum take them, so they couldn't be dangerous. She didn't do danger – apart from marrying his dad, that is.

Angel had spent the night on the streets, curled up in an old armchair someone had thrown out on to the pavement. Luckily it had been warm, although he'd woken up stiff and ice-cold, like something you'd just taken out of the freezer. All night long, whenever he'd opened his eyes, he could see the lights in his flat, twentieth floor, second from the left. That's where he'd been heading when he'd left Poppy's. Thought he'd risk it at home, although his head was so muzzy he hardly knew what he was doing.

Trouble was, when he'd got up outside the lift and was skulking along the corridor to his flat, he'd nearly been squashed by two ambulance men running past him. He'd heard the sirens earlier but taken no notice. There was always a siren for one reason or another. He wouldn't have taken much notice of the medics except that one of them knocked his bad arm.

Next thing, when he was standing back dozily recovering, they went past again half-carrying a lady. And that lady was his mum!

Like that wasn't shock enough, next thing that big fat Eloise comes out shrieking, 'My sister! She dying! Oh my sister! She dying!'

He was prepared to believe her, what with his mum looking so odd and the ambulance men and all. But one of them called back, 'She's not dying, Madam, she's having a baby.' And his mate added softly, 'If you're bright enough to tell the difference.'

Eloise wasn't bright enough to light up a pinhead, in Angel's opinion, but anyway she was yelling far too loudly to hear what anyone else was saying. Besides which, she had Gabriel in her arms and he was bawling out at the top of his lungs: 'Mama! Mama! Mama!'

No sign of his dad, of course.

Unsure what to do, Angel had hovered for a moment, before deciding to follow the ambulance men. He caught up with them just as they were putting his mum into the ambulance.

'Mum! It's me, Angel.'

She'd turned her head and even smiled a little. 'Angel. Just in time to see me off.' Quite calm, she'd been. 'Next time you see me I'll have another babe in my arms,' she'd added, just before they closed the doors.

The medic then turned to him. 'You all right, son?'

'No way,' was the right answer. Instead he said, 'Cheers, mate,' and slipped off into the darkness.

He stood there and watched the ambulance go off, his head whirling about like the light on its roof. When it was quiet again, he leant against the wall. Another baby. Nice for some! His mum had looked really happy, if a bit anxious, as well she might with that stupid sister shrieking that she was dying.

There was no way he was going into the flat with Eloise there. So that's how he'd ended up in the smelly old armchair, watching the lights of his flat. Fate was against him, man. Big Time.

Since getting up, he'd been circling the estate,

watching for Eloise coming out. She was well capable of leaving the kids on their own if she needed a trip out. Then he'd dive in when she wasn't around. Food, that's what he needed. A brother can't live on pills alone. Ever since he'd been stabbed, he'd no appetite at all, so it might be a good thing he was feeling hungry. Maybe he was getting better. But it wasn't such a good thing being hungry if you didn't have any food. If felt like a rat was gnawing at his stomach.

What with his dizzy head, his leaden arm and a rat in his stomach, he wasn't doing too well. The other problem was Snake. He supposed he should have waited for Poppy and the others to come back with the news. He wasn't thinking straight, that was the truth. He'd done his growing up under the flyover, and even he found it nipped his heart sometimes. 'Never rely on others,' that's what his dad had taught him. 'Even your brothers will let you down.'

True. True. You aren't called Snake for nothing. Thinking of the Flyers made him remember that raid on the supermarket. They'd come out with a bottle of vodka. Easy. No one after them. What did supermarkets have? Food. What did he need? Food. What didn't he have? Money.

Up until that moment Angel had been meandering, hood up, eyes down, not seeing and not wanting to be seen. Now he changed direction and squared his shoulders. The supermarket was at the bottom of one of the high-rises next to the one with the scaffolding.

He'd just walk in, no hood – they didn't let boys in with hoods up. His mum sent him there shopping most days. They wouldn't suspect him. He wouldn't go for anything big. Just a packet of biscuits. The shelf was near the door. He'd walk out through it with the biscuits. Easy. The rat in his stomach would be cheering him on.

Angel moved quickly.

Poppy arrived at the estate. In the daylight and with no drama-queen Jude at her side it seemed much less frightening. She still thought it was a horrible place to live. The buildings were so tall – ugly tall, not like skyscrapers in New York or somewhere – and they were even scruffier than they'd seemed at night. There were men working on the one covered in scaffolding. As she watched, a little box – a lift, she supposed – was coming down the outside of the building, all forty floors. One scary ride!

Poppy looked down at the map Will had given her. Angel's flat was in the outer building furthest from the motorways. The roads stretched out above and behind the estate, a black cat's cradle of crossings and recrossings with the continual movement of traffic like a necklace of different-coloured beads, some glittering like diamonds in the sunlight. Pity they made such a horrible noise. She remembered how dark it had been underneath, and shivered.

Slowly she set off towards Angel's block. To cheer herself, she pictured Seraphina and Gabriel, Angel's kid sister and brother. At least they weren't scary.

Angel stood just inside the supermarket. He wished his head would stop spinning. It wasn't very big, but the lights and shelves confused him.

'Can I help you?' A girl was staring at him.

'No. No.' He brushed past her. There were the biscuits, a whole row of them, with cakes and sweets beside them. Perhaps he'd have chocolate instead. Supposed to be good for you, that bitter dark stuff. He tried to stay calm. Take something, take anything, he told himself, then have a look to see nobody's near and walk out casually, like you've paid. His legs felt so wobbly, that was the trouble.

Very carefully, Angel reached out to the shelf. Without realising it, he'd shut his eyes (if you can't see other people, they can't see you) until his left hand (right hand out of action) lighted on a cake. He withdrew his hand and opened his eyes. Ginger. He hated ginger. No time to change it now.

Swaying unsteadily and keeping close to the shelves, he edged his way towards the door.

'Hey! You, boy!'

The voice was so loud and angry that Poppy stopped and turned round to see who was shouting. It was a short burly man with a girl at his side, standing in front of a supermarket. They were both staring in the same direction, so Poppy did too.

At first, all she could see was a group of workmen in orange helmets and jackets. They were coming out of a lift which had just reached ground level.

'Get that boy!' yelled the burly man. 'He stole from my shop!'

''Yeah, catch him!' shrieked the girl.

The workmen hesitated.

'That way!' screamed the man. 'Behind you! I can't leave the shop.'

'Behind you!' squealed the girl.

Now people were appearing from all sides. They stood staring, most of them smiling.

'I've rung the police!' bawled the burly man whose lungs matched his girth.

'Police on their way!' shrieked the girl. The men in orange spread out and began to run in different directions.

Even though Poppy knew stealing was wrong, she began to feel sorry for the burglar, whoever it was. The odds were so stacked against him.

Now there was a police siren wailing and four or five policemen came to join the chase.

'They'll get him now, poor sod,' said a woman with a push chair who was standing beside Poppy.

'I suppose he shouldn't steal...' said Poppy tentatively. But the woman had turned to greet a friend.

It was surprising they still hadn't caught him – if it was a 'he', which everyone seemed to think. More and more people, attracted by the police siren, had come out to watch and suddenly there was a shout. It came from one of the workmen.

'He's in the lift!'

Every face turned towards the little glass box and for a moment there was silence as the lift began to move upwards.

Then everybody started talking at once. 'It's a boy in there. Can't be more than twelve or thirteen.'

'They've scared him into doing something silly.'

'Big bullies!'

'He won't know how to work it.'

'What are those workmen doing, leaving it operational?'

'Irresponsible.'

'A menace to all of us.'

'And how long have they been messing about with that building?'

'It's an accident waiting to happen.'

'Poor lad.'

As they spoke, everybody kept their eyes fixed on the lift which was moving slowly but surely up the side of the building. A small figure was just visible inside. The women and children surrounding Poppy all seemed to be having a good time, even though they went on about 'the poor lad' and 'the cruel danger'.

She turned to the woman with the pushchair who'd spoken to her earlier. 'Do you know who's in there?'

'Jade!' the woman called to her friend who was now chatting with someone else as well as scolding her two sons. 'It's Maria's son, isn't it?'

'She's off having her baby so that sister's in charge.' The friend called back. 'That's what Sammy said – he saw the boy running out of the shop. Only took a cake, and he dropped that. Sammy grabbed it quick so there was no evidence.'

The women carried on talking among themselves. Although Poppy didn't know Angel's mum's name, a horrible feeling was making her so tense she almost forgot to breathe. Angel's mum was pregnant, wasn't she? She hardly wanted to hear more but couldn't resist listening.

'Maria's a lovely girl, but what can she do with that husband?' said one woman.

'Lost her first son to a bullet, didn't she, and now the next's going the same way,' contributed another.

'And what a sister,' said the third. 'More boobs than brains. What's she called? Something fancy.'

They all thought for a moment before the first woman announced triumphantly, 'Eloise!'

Poppy gave a little scream, went red, then white, and nearly fainted. It was Angel with his hurt arm in that little glass box halfway up the side of the building. If something went wrong, he would drop like a stone to the ground.

'We've got to do something!' she shouted, 'He's hurt his arm! He's got a temperature! We've got to get him out of there!'

The women stopping talking and turned to her with curious, sympathetic faces.

'Friend of yours, is he, love?' An older woman came over and put an arm round Poppy. She was warm and smelled of chips because she was holding a carton in her other hand. Poppy found herself clinging on to her as if she was her mum instead of some random woman.

'He's a friend from school,' she whispered

'Is he now? We'll have to see he's all right, then. I'm Maggie, and here's a chip to cheer you up.'

'Look, Mum,' yelled an excited little boy, 'he's heading for the top.'

Chapter Eleven

Angel stood in the glass box with his left hand pressed on the button that kept it going upwards. He was beyond being frightened and felt as if he was in some kind of time machine so that when he finally stopped and stepped out, he'd be in another world. Which, all things considered, wouldn't be a bad thing.

He didn't want to look down because it made him feel even sicker than he did already. He couldn't believe he'd been sad enough to drop the ginger cake; even if he didn't like the taste, it would have made him feel less odd and floaty. Maybe he *was* floating and not in a glass box at all. He must get a grip. Not floating. On one side, there was a great deal of fresh air and a fine view of the motorways, and on the other side, floor after floor swathed in green netting and steel scaffolding. This was real, man.

In a way he wished the trip would never end.

He'd left it all behind, hadn't he. Safe from the police, safe from Snake, safe from his dad, safe from everything and everybody. What a story!

Just as Angel was beginning to enjoy himself, there was a jolt and the lift stopped.

Angel looked out. Where there had been building, now there was just sky. It took him a moment to realise that he'd reached the top. He was staring across the roof. A very wide, very flat roof.

He pushed open the door and stumbled out. He stood still, gasping at the air and at the height – he was far higher than the motorway, maybe as high as an aeroplane – not that he'd ever been in one. And, get a grip, man, a plane would have to fly higher than the building or it would hit it. Perhaps a bird, then.

Angel began to giggle weakly. If he wasn't careful, he'd lose his marbles. All the same, it was just about the most exciting place he'd ever been. Swaying like a drunk, he left the lift and went over to the edge of the roof.

Down below, like little gnomes, he could see crowds of people – staring up at him, probably. He could pick out the feds in their white shirts and the workmen in their orange helmets. He wondered if Eloise was there. It'd serve her right if she suffered a bit of worry over him – not that it was very likely. Cow!

Suddenly amidst the mass of faces he saw a blob of bright orange, which wasn't a workman's helmet because it moved.

'Poppy!' called Angel. But his words only reached down a few floors before they blew away.

Angel stepped closer to the edge. He would have liked someone up here with him. More fun. He lifted up his good arm to wave to the orange hair. There was so much sky around him that he felt like a bird. Or an angel. Angels fly, don't they. He slowly lifted up the other arm as far as it would go without hurting. Maybe he could fly down to her.

'Hey, you!'

He'd been hearing distant noises from ground level, sirens mainly, but this was different, close by. On the roof. He turned round dizzily.

'You want to step back a pace or two. Unless you're planning to join the great blue yonder.'

Angel stared. The man speaking wore a hard hat but he didn't look like your average workman. Too old, for one thing. He was small, in a singlet, very sinewy with brown leathery skin and eyes that, even from this distance, Angel could tell were a brilliant blue.

'Name's Angel. I was thinking of flying.'

'Were you just.' The man took off his hat, revealing stiff white hair sticking up like a brush, and came closer. 'So if your name was Sugar, you'd be looking for a cup of tea.'

'Nobody's called Sugar.'

'That's where you're wrong, sonny boy. Never heard of Sugar Ray Robinson? World-famous boxer.'

'Anyway, I wasn't planning to jump.' Angel took a few steps back from the edge. 'You're not police, are you?'

'Not me. Not my favourite gents, although they have their uses. Climbing up forty floors when the lift's shut down isn't one of them. You won't get the men in blue up here in a hurry. I was on the roof already.'

'You're a workman, then?'

'Not that neither. Hey, do you mind if we sit down? I've never had much of a head for heights.'

'If I sit down,' said Angel, sitting down. 'I'll probably fall asleep. I haven't been in bed for three nights.'

The man crouched down beside him. 'I'm Gus,' he said, holding out his hand.

It was strange shaking hands on the top of a high-rise when the police were after you and your head was spinning. 'Ouch.'

'Bad arm, have you? I noticed that.'

'Like I got stabbed.' Angel looked to see how Gus reacted, but he only smiled.

'That wasn't very clever.'

'Then I hid, then I stole a cake. That's why I'm up here. On the run.'

'Seems you're in need of help. I'll tell you what, why don't you tell me the whole story from the beginning?' Gus's blue eyes peered at Angel in a bright, enquiring way.

Angel didn't know why he trusted the little old man but he began talking at once, telling him everything that had happened to him, including his dad's history, his horrible aunt Eloise, his mum's new baby, Snake and the brothers who weren't such good brothers, hiding at Poppy's and then having this rat gnawing at his stomach but no money which is why he stole the cake. He told the story in fits and starts because he felt so strange and weak. Sometimes he paused, Gus intervened.

'Snake, did you say? I know him. He's one sad boy. Sleeps out there under the flyover 'cause his stepdad beats him. That's why he beats you up, you smaller lads. Makes him feel big.'

When Angel told him about Poppy, he commented, 'So that's who you were shouting to.'

'Yeah,' Angel half-closed his eyes. 'I saw her down there.'

When he hadn't said anything more for several minutes, Gus sat up straight. 'So what are we going to do about you? That's some big question.'

'Umh.' Angel slumped down further. 'Can't I just stay up here?'

'That's an option. I won't say it's not an option.' Gus paused for thought. 'Do you play football?'

'I kick a ball,' mumbled Angel. He opened his eyes again, but it felt as if the sky was about to drop on his head so he shut them again.

'I run a football game under the flyover. Gives the boys something to do. Under-fourteens on Saturday. Big boys on Sunday. We could do with a strapping lad like you.'

Angel flapped his hand wearily. 'My arm hurts.'

'Fullback. That's where I'd start you. Training sessions, fitness, diet. I look after my boys. Strikes me you need someone to look after you. I used to be a boxer, bantam weight, then a boxing trainer, but everyone wants football these days.'

Angel had stopped listening. He'd just remember the paracetamol. He pulled the packet out of his pocket.

'Hey, what have you got there, son?' Wiry fingers reached over and grabbed the packet. 'You're not taking these, are you?'

'They're to stop the pain,' muttered Angel, trying to grab the packet back.

Gus was suddenly agitated, 'How many have you taken?'

'I don't know, do I.' Now when Angel opened his eyes there were strange red and green blotches dancing about. 'I need to keep still, don't I.'

'No, you don't. What we need is a hospital.'

'My arm's not that bad. It's my head.'

'It's not your arm or your head I'm worried about. Too many of these and you die, got it?'

Angel didn't get it, because at that moment everything caught up with him and he passed out, lying flat on the tarmac roof like an old rag.

Gus bent over him, felt his head and wrist and then sat back. 'Now, Gus old man, this is the time to prove you've got some muscles left in this scrawny old body of yours.'

Chapter Twelve

At ground level, the crowd had grown even bigger. There was even a television camera with a huge long lens that could see better than any human what was happening up on the roof.

Poppy, with her new friend Maggie, edged over to hear what the camera man was saying. The worst moment was when he pronounced calmly, 'I think he's going to jump.'

But a few minutes later he added, 'There's someone up there with him. Looks like another child or a small man.'

At this news, the police rushed over to the workmen to ask who could be up there, and after a lot of scratching of heads one of them suddenly remembered that a local man, someone involved in community work, had persuaded them to take him up. He'd wanted to look out for a new ground for his football club or something like that. They'd quite forgotten to bring him down so he must still be up there.

'Does he have white sticking-up hair?' a policeman asked the cameraman.

'Sure does. Hold on! Looks like there's movement.'

Maggie, who was exceptionally good at overhearing other people's conversations, pinched Poppy's arm. 'That'll be Gus. Told you he'd be OK. Gus is like a dad to half the bad boys on the estate already.'

'Angel isn't bad,' began Poppy indignantly. 'At least, he doesn't want to be bad.' She caught Maggie's smile. 'He just gets into trouble.'

'Don't you worry, love,' Maggie put an arm round her shoulders. 'Now look up there. If I'm not mistaken, the lift has started on its way down.'

All heads were turned in the same direction. Quite distinctly, the lift began to make its descent.

'That's that, then,' said a woman with startling purple hair, 'Show's over. He's coming down, the police will take him off to the station, and I'm off to make tea.'

A lot of the crowd seemed to agree with Purple Hair because they began to drift away. It struck Poppy that she should be going too, if she didn't want to be found out by Jude and her mum.

Instead, she followed Maggie to where the police and the workmen were waiting for the lift to reach the ground.

It was already halfway down and they could see inside, although not clearly. 'There's Gus!' exclaimed Maggie excitedly. She waved her hands as if she expected him to wave back. 'But I can't see your mate.' She screwed up her brown eyes.

'Nor can I.' Poppy screwed up her eyes too.

'I'll tell you what, don't know why nobody's thought of it' – Maggie scrabbled in the huge pink bag she was carrying over her arm – 'I'll give him a call.' She triumphantly produced her mobile, which was decorated with photos of Matt Dillon.

Everybody could see Gus reaching in his pocket.

'Hi, Gus. It's Maggie. How's the boy?... Paracetamol and a bad arm?' She was speaking loudly enough for one of the police to overhear. He came over and held out his hand for the mobile, but Maggie kept it pressed to her ear. 'Ambulance, not police.'

She shut the phone and announced, 'He's out cold. Maybe an overdose, or fever or hunger or the lot of them. What he needs is a doctor.' She stood there challenging the police.

Poppy thought that with her large body clad in

yellow and turquoise, her shiny black hair and her determined manner, no one would dare say no to Maggie. Clearly, her motherly nature disguised a steely core.

Sure enough, the policeman, who only looked about fifteen, took up his mobile and rang for an ambulance.

'There you are,' said Maggie. 'I told you he'd be fine.'

'He doesn't sound very fine,' said Poppy doubtfully.

'They'll deal with his problems. Don't you worry. Boys recover in a flash. I should know, with six sons and ten grandsons. Come on now, the lift's just about down.'

Poppy watched, holding her breath, as the glass box dropped the last few feet and landed with a jerk at the bottom.

Immediately the door opened and a little man, brown and wrinkled, but very active, jumped out. Then she could see Angel lying on the floor.

'Angel! Angel!' She rushed forward but before she could reach him, a policeman put out an arm.

'Stop there, love.'

'He's my friend. Angel!' She called even more

frantically, and was near enough to see him open his eyes.

'Poppy...' He pulled himself up.

Gus, who was talking to another policeman, looked from Poppy to Angel. 'There.' His blue eyes were bright and kindly. 'You've worked a miracle. Go on. Say hi, before the doctor gets hold of him.' He turned away from them. 'That's the ambulance now, by the sound of that siren.'

'So he won't die?' whispered Poppy, so Angel wouldn't hear.

'Course not. He'll be right as rain tomorrow. Go on. Say a word in his ear before it's too late.'

So Poppy, with Maggie close behind her, knelt beside Angel. 'I was terrified,' she said. Suddenly she felt cross. 'What were you doing?'

'Great views from the top!' whispered Angel. 'I'll take you up some time.'

'No, thank you,' said Poppy firmly.

'I was going to fly down to you but my arm hurt. You haven't got anything to eat, have you? I'm starving. Got a rat in my stomach.'

'What are you talking about?'

'Gnawing at me. Hunger. That's what it feels like.'

'Gus said you took a lot of paracetamol. Did you?'

asked Poppy suspiciously.

'Gus is my guardian angel. He's coming with me to the hospital.'

'You don't seem too bad to me.'

'Make way for the stretcher,' bellowed a voice behind them.

'I can walk,' objected Angel, and stood up to prove it. But even Poppy could see how weak and trembly he was.

She watched as two men in green overalls put Angel on a stretcher and carried him to the ambulance. Gus stayed close and got in the ambulance with him. The doors closed.

Maggie stood beside Poppy. 'Just been told that his mum's in the same hospital having a baby. They can have a family reunion, can't they?' She laughed, then took Poppy's hand. 'Now you'd better be going home. You're not from the estate, are you?'

'I'm only a few streets away.' Poppy hesitated. 'I didn't bring my mobile, but if I give you the number, would you tell me how he is? I'll be at school so it'll have to be after four.'

Maggie began rummaging in her huge bag again. 'He's a lucky lad to have a caring friend like you.' She pulled out the mobile and held it ready. 'Fire ahead.'

After Poppy had given the number, she walked slowly away. There were still a few people gathered outside the supermarket but most of the crowd had gone. No one took any notice of her and she suddenly felt lonely.

She walked faster. Maybe she'd get back without being missed. She felt as if she'd been away for days, but when she looked at her watch it wasn't even two hours. The sun was still high.

She went round the back of Jude's house where she knew there was a key under a dustbin and let herself directly into the garden. Everything was just as she'd left it. So peaceful. Like another world, even though she'd only come a short distance. The swing seat was now in the shade but her mobile was just where she'd left it.

Two messages. The first from Jude: 'We're late. Aunt Virginia has made a special chocolate cake so we have to stay for tea. Hope you're having a nice quiet time.' No, thought Poppy. Not nice – terrifying. Not quiet – filled with sirens and shouting.

The other message was a text from Will. 'What news Angel?'

'Good,' Poppy texted back. 'In hospital.' She'd tell him more tomorrow. She sat down on the swing seat and felt a crackle in her pocket.

The letter from her dad! She still hadn't opened it. Too much going on. But did she really want to? It was addressed to her mum. On the other hand, perhaps it was her duty, since her mum was away, to see what he wanted.

My darling Irena, my princess,' the letter began, which was totally embarrassing. Poppy skipped on quickly, noticing in passing how cramped and awkward the handwriting was, so different from her dad's flamboyant behaviour. Probably it was because he was left-handed. Funny, the things you learnt about your dad when he wasn't there.

'Today I had the best news. I nearly rang but needed to put it in writing so we can both believe it's true. The authorities that be have decided to move me to an open prison. Now, before you get too excited, 'open' doesn't mean I'm free. I'm still in prison, locked up at nights and subject to all sorts of conditions, but I can work outside. I'll even get what's called 'home leave', days and later on, weekends when I can actually come to you. Oh, darling beautiful Irena…'

Poppy folded up the letter and firmly put it back into the envelope. She'd tell her mum because it would make her happy. Just at the moment, she found it hard to take in.

'Poppy! Poppy! Where are you?' It was a relief when she heard Jude's voice from the house. 'Oh, there you are.' She stood by the garden door. 'Aren't you cold out there?' Without waiting for an answer, she held up something in her hand and cried out, 'Come and see what my aunt gave me!'

Feeling stiff and cramped, Poppy went to her.

'Look. An iPod with four apps on it already. The one I like best is Rooftop Chase. Here, you can have a go if you want.'

Poppy tried to focus on the little screen. She pressed a button and watched as little figures zigzagged at wild speed, then leapt into the air.

'Control it,' directed Jude excitedly. 'The aim is to jump from rooftop to rooftop. I've notched up eight levels.'

Poppy looked more closely and abruptly handed the iPod back to Jude. 'I'm hungry. I haven't had any tea.'

At that moment, the one thing she didn't want to look at was a small figure on top of a very tall building.

Chapter Thirteen

It was the first day of the new term. Poppy and Jude were walking briskly to school and Jude's mother was with them, helping with their bags.

'It's still hot.' She looked up at the blue sky. 'But rain's forecast so I've put in your raincoats.'

'Uhm,' said Jude.

'Uhm,' said Poppy. Then she too stared upwards. Ever since she'd woken up that morning, she'd had the image of Angel standing on the edge of the high-rise stuck in her head. She glanced at Jude. It was odd to have a best friend who you couldn't tell things to. She suspected Jude was longing to meet up with the other girls in the school, Amber for one. Amber liked sport and was sensible and certainly didn't have bad boyfriends.

'I wonder if Will is coming,' Poppy said out loud.

'Probably ill.' Jude sounded bored.

But Will was there. He and Poppy gave each other impatient looks across the classroom and the moment the bell went for break, they ran outside together.

'What happened?' began Will, as soon as they were in the playground. 'Did you tell Angel about Snake?'

'What?' Poppy looked startled. In all the drama of yesterday she had quite forgotten about Snake. 'Actually, I never got a chance to talk about Snake.'

'But that was the whole point of you going to find Angel!' Will sounded shocked and cross.

Poppy, who had been longing to tell everything to Will, wondered how she could even begin. 'The thing is, I didn't exactly find him. When I arrived on the estate, he'd stolen a cake from the supermarket and the police were after him.'

'Oh, no!' Will groaned. 'Did they get him?'

'He escaped into a workman's lift that went up the side of that tall building with the scaffolding. He went all the way to the top…' As Poppy told the story, she watched Will's pale face mirror her own terror. 'It was the most frightening thing I've ever seen,' she ended. 'Worse than Snake grabbing me. When he got to the bottom again safely I felt like bursting into tears. And that was the only moment I got to talk to him. So you can see why I didn't think of saying anything about Snake.'

'Sounds like it wasn't in Angel's head any more either.' Will nodded sympathetically. 'So what now?' He looked at Poppy with bright, eager eyes.

Poppy had always found Will's keenness for adventures rather irritating when illness so often stopped him taking part in them. But she did want to tell him about Maggie. 'There's this woman, Maggie, who looked after me. Old. She's got hoards of children and grandchildren. She's going to ring me with news about Angel.'

'That's good.' Will put his hands together like a wise old man. 'You will tell me, won't you?'

'I've no one else.' Poppy tried not to sound sorry for herself.

'Thanks for the compliment.' Will smiled to show he wasn't offended, although he probably was.

The first day of a new term always seemed long, but this one seemed endless to Poppy. At last the final bell rang and she joined the rush for the cloakroom and the school gates. Maggie might ring at any time. She had her mobile ready in her pocket.

'Hey, Poppy!'

Poppy whirled round. She couldn't believe her ears. And then her eyes. There, skirting along a corner of the railings, was Angel! He had his arm in a sling but otherwise looked quite his normal self.

'Angel!' Poppy hurried over. 'What are you doing here? Are you all right?'

'Hey, man. How d'you rate my sling?' Angel stood in his usual confident slouch as if the last few days had never happened.

'Better than my bandage, have to admit.' Poppy tried to imitate his carefree manner. 'The hospital kicked you out, did they?'

'Best night's sleep I ever had. Out cold, once they'd sorted my arm. Didn't even have to pump out my stomach. Strong, man. Slept from eight to eight. Would have slept another eight if they'd let me.'

'So you really are all right?'

'Took my temperature – for the knowledge, thirty-seven is normal – gave me a jab or two and by lunchtime Gus and I were on the move.'

'Gus? Oh, the old man.'

'He's not that old. Plenty of muscles. Carried me to the lift, so he told me,' Angel smiled cheerfully. 'He's going to enrol me in his football team once my arm's better.'

'But what about that cake you stole?'

'Like, is that the question of a friend?' For the first time, Angel looked a little less pleased with himself. 'If you're so keen to know, the shopman didn't press charges. You know what that means?'

'Of course I do!' Poppy thought she deserved a better line from Angel, considering all the help she'd given him.

'So the feds aren't after me. I'm free.' He started to wave his arms, then made a face and quickly lowerd his bad arm.

'I'm glad you're free,' said Poppy stiffly, 'but some of us have homework to do and we might even have to scrub blood off certain floors.'

'Hey, don't take it like that. I give you gratitude. Respect. I tell you the good news. Life isn't easy. My mum's in hospital with no baby yet which leaves Eloise in the home none too pleased with me…'

'I've got to go, Angel, or we'll have Jude over here, and she's not too pleased with you either, and I haven't even told her about the cake…'

'It was ginger. I don't care for ginger.'

'Poor you…' Poppy began to move away, before she remembered something else. 'And you stole my mum's paracetamol.'

'Mistake. I admit it. Bad mistake. I could've killed myself. Saved your mum from that, didn't I.'

'My mum would never be stupid enough to take too many.'

Poppy started away again in what she hoped was a dignified manner. Wouldn't he say sorry for anything?

'And there's another thing!' Poppy couldn't believe she'd nearly forgotten Snake again. She went back to Angel. 'Will, Jude and me went under the flyover and found your gang and that disgusting Snake – and you've never even asked about it. I suppose it doesn't matter that he snatched me and I might have been stabbed, too, or worse. Like, like, murdered! You don't care about me at all. My life isn't easy either, you know. Maybe I'll be like Jude and not have you as a friend any more!'

Poppy stopped. She was bright red in the face and very cross. She half-expected Angel to run away, but he stood in front of her looking down and scuffing the ground with his feet. She noticed, irrelevantly, that they weren't the top-of-the-range sort he usually wore.

'Yeah,' he mumbled, without looking up. 'The

bro can be rough. I say thank you for going there. Gus gave me a new line on Snake. Not all his fault. You know, he bullies because his stepdad bullies him.'

'Thanks for that. I'll remember that when he grabs me next time. Not that there'll be a next time.' Poppy swung round to check on Jude and to her surprise saw there was no one left waiting outside the gates. Jude must have gone without her. That figured.

'Hey. One bit of news.'

Poppy turned back to Angel who was still not looking at her properly. 'I've been put in care,' he muttered.

'What do you mean?' said Poppy impatiently. He was mumbling so badly, she could hardly hear a word.

'Eloise won't have me at home. Not that I want to be with her, neither. But I'll miss Seraphina and Gabriel. She says she can't control me. Nor can she. Fat cow.'

'So where will you live?'

'In a foster family. I went to the same place once before. When my mum had Gabriel.'

Poppy pushed her hair off her hot face and thought for a moment. 'Like me, then. Living with another family. Mum away.'

'Suppose.' Angel didn't sound convinced.

'What about your dad? Is he in prison at the moment like mine?' As she spoke, Poppy remembered Big Frank was soon going to this thing called an 'open prison' but she didn't feel like talking about it.

Angel aimed a kick at the railings. 'Could be anywhere, my dad. Wouldn't mind living with him, though.'

'Why don't you, then?' said Poppy abstractedly. She needed to go.

'Told you. Don't know where he is. They'd never let me, anyway.'

'Who are "they"?' Poppy asked, but didn't wait for an answer.

Angel watched her go. He was in no hurry. It was good not to feel sick any more. Like normal. Just a throb in his arm. Couldn't ride a bike, though. If he had a bike. Which he didn't. His dad took it off him last time he was around. Said he could turn it into cash. And cash meant more cash. Took the iPod he'd given him on his last visit. Took his mobile too, even though it had gone down the day before. No toys left, man. That's what his mum said. Mum in hospital and out of sight. Didn't even see her when he was in hospital himself.

Angel kicked the pavement again, then watched as a drop of water hit the toe of his trainer fair and square. Rain. It hadn't rained for ever. Time for tea.

❧

Poppy was speaking to her mum. Or trying to. Actually, her mum was speaking to her. She was sounding very Polish, which must be because she was in the country she grew up in.

'Your grandmama is in the ground. Today. The Mass so beautiful, and I wish you there.'

'So, Mum, now you can come back!'

Irena didn't seem to hear. 'Your grandpapa is so sad, he cries. An old man with tears falling on his dear cheeks…'

'Mum, there's a letter from Big Frank.'

'He needs me so much like a little lost boy…'

Poppy tried again. 'Dad needs you. I need you.'

Irena seemed to be paying a little more attention. 'Oh, yes. Oh, yes. Your poor papa, locked up, but he will understand.' She sighed sorrowfully. 'And you, my darling daughter, and my little music students. All need me. But now I must be here with duty to my father. You understand?'

'Yes, Mum.' Poppy gave up trying to tell her about Big Frank and the open prison. Maybe in a few days.

From outside she heard Jude calling that tea was ready. Maybe she'd write back to her dad.

Angel ate his tea – chicken nuggets and beans on toast – in his foster family's living room. He had to use his left hand, spiking each nugget and each bean with a fork. Gave him something to do, didn't it. Sky sports was on television – cricket because Rob, the man of the house, liked cricket. England was beating Sir Lanka and every now and again Rob rose in his chair and yelled, 'Yes!'

'Can't we have football?' muttered Angel.

'Not the season.' Rob didn't take his eyes from the screen.

But there was always football somewhere. When they'd been waiting in the hospital, Gus told him his lads played all summer. The carer woman had said this was the best foster family for him because there was a man as a role model. Good thinking – if they wanted him to turn into a TV potato. One arm of Rob's chair was greasy and dented where he leant on it watching TV.

Lee-Anne, his wife, was all right. She did the boring stuff, even smiled, asked how he was. They were professional carers, so being nice was probably part of the deal. They got paid thousands.

Last time he'd been there every bedroom was filled: four boys, three of them older than him. They'd got up to all sorts. Lee-Anne had certainly earned her money. But this time there was no one else there. Boring, man. Rob told him they were only into emergency fostering now, which is why he was there. Not a good scene. He'd be looking forward to school soon. But that didn't start for a week – later than normal school.

Angel pushed aside his plate and stood up. Rob's eyes never left the screen. He wasn't supposed to be out after six. Slowly he moved towards the door. It had stopped raining. Why not go and look up Gus in his football ground? Wouldn't mind him as a male role model. He eased the door open and was through it just as Rob gave a 'Ye-e-e-s!' That would keep him busy for a while. As long as Lee-Anne stayed in the kitchen. Angel didn't have a door key but it was their job to let him in, wasn't it. Any time.

Outside, the rain had made the air fresher and the streets cleaner. Angel kicked away a plastic bottle. He walked quickly, skirting the edge of the estate so he wouldn't meet anyone he knew. Just in case, he pulled over his hood. Looking up, he could hardly believe he'd stood on the top of one of those buildings. Crazy, man. He gave himself respect, even if he had been halfway out of his mind.

Once he was under the roads, he slowed down. He liked the feeling of all that power and speed over his head. When he'd made his fortune he'd drive a Maserati – red, probably, or maybe gold or ice-blue.

He was picturing himself at the wheel of a red Maserati when he looked up and saw, walking just a few yards ahead, with his back to him but easily recognisable, Snake. He seemed to be on his own.

Angel hesitated. He could easily duck out of sight or make a dash for Gus's football ground where he could already hear kids shouting, but something held him to the spot. Why should he run away? If he ran away now, he'd be running for the rest of his life.

At that moment Snake, as if feeling the eyes boring

into his back, turned round. Casually, with a long, slow stride, he advanced towards Angel.

'Heard your story, bro.' He came closer.

'What story?' Angel was confused. Stabbing him was something Snake did, not heard. There was an odd expression on his face which Angel couldn't place.

'All over the estate. Up in the lift to the top. Some joyride!'

Angel realised that Snake's usually snarling face was now expressing admiration.

'Awesome, man. Made the feds look like boiled ants.'

Angel tried to look modest. 'It was nothing, bro.' Next thing, Snake would be apologising for stabbing him!

'That's some bandage,' said Snake.

'It's a sling. Had a night in hospital.'

'Shouldn't have done that.'

'Brothers fight,' said Angel forgivingly, and looked with surprise as Snake offered him a roll-up. He must have made an impression, for Snake would as soon give away his precious knife as smokes. Angel shook his head and turned slightly away, listening for the noise of the football game.

Snake looked too. 'You're not playing there, man. Not with that arm.'

'I came down from the roof with him. Gus.'

Snake frowned. 'Yeah. He's one determined man. Take over your life before you know it.'

Angel moved restlessly, clasping and unclasping the fingers of the hand poking out of the sling. He thought he'd rather have his life taken over by Gus than Snake. Funny, that. Before, when he'd been scared by Snake's big talk and big style, he'd wanted to be one of his bros, and now, when Snake was looking at him like a hero, he'd lost interest. 'Got to thank Gus,' he said, moving away.

Snake's grey eyes flickered in a not-good way. Then Angel remembered: things change, but a snake is always a snake. He raised his left hand in salute and set off towards the football ground.

When he'd gone a few paces, he heard Snake calling him. 'I had something to say to you, man.' His tone of voice had changed, just like his eyes. Not a pretty sight.

Angel turned. 'Say it.'

'You don't want my company. Am I right?' Snake was swaying slightly from side to side, a bit like a snake before it strikes.

'I'm leaving,' agreed Angel, remembering the argument that had ended with his stabbing. It had been nothing: standing in 'Snake space' – that sort of stupid nothing. But Snake had looked at him then, swaying like that.

'What is it?' he said. 'Something big?'

'Snake shrugged. 'Big for some.' He smiled a little. 'But you're leaving me. You don't need to know.'

'Tell me,' said Angel, trying to stay calm.

'Don't think I will do that,' Snake swayed forward, 'now that you don't want my company.'

'Don't, then!' yelled Angel, suddenly losing his cool, and he started walking, almost running, towards the football ground. He wasn't going to play games with Snake and he wasn't going to be stabbed by him either. Probably he had nothing to tell him. Just wanted to cause trouble.

When he arrived at the ground, the game was finished and the players were clustering round Gus. Angel, trying to recover his cool, hung back until Gus spotted him.

'So here's the high-rise explorer! Lads, meet Angel, who was planning on flying two hundred feet up.'

Angel recognised a few of the faces, who mostly said 'Hi,' or nodded unenthusiastically in his direction. He didn't expect more. New boy, wasn't he.

'So how long shall we give your arm?' said Gus, who was just about the smallest person there. 'Two weeks? Three weeks?'

Angel's face showed the disappointment he felt. 'It's fine.'

'Can't risk it, son.'

'Just needs a day or two.'

'That's not what the hospital told me. Time passes. I'll come and see you. At Rob's and Lee-Anne's, aren't you?'

'Uhm,' agreed Angel, watching Gus turn his attention back to the players.

Two or three weeks! When he thought he'd found someone who cared.

As Angel walked home (some kind of home!) it began to rain again. He banged on the front door and had time to think about the notice stuck there, 'No flyers' – that didn't mean him, presumably – before Lee-Anne came to open it.

'There you are,' she said in a not unfriendly way. 'I can't chase after you, you know.' They came together into the hallway. Angel looked through into the living room and saw that Rob was in exactly the same position as before, eyes fixed on the TV.

'If I had a mobile, you could call me. You wouldn't be worried then.' Which was a stupid remark because Lee-Anne hadn't looked at all worried.

Lee-Anne's turned back made it clear that mobiles weren't her concern. 'You'll be in your school next week,' she said over her shoulder. 'Then you'll have something to keep you busy.'

Angel lay on his bed, arms at his side, like a corpse. He'd stick it out where he was for a day or two, so everybody thought he was settled, then do a runner. Anywhere would be better than this way of death.

Chapter Fourteen

Poppy picked up yet another letter from her dad. He was over the moon! Out already! Well, in an open prison. Why hadn't Irena written? No, wait – of course. Her letter would have gone to Her Majesty's Prison, Castlerock, and now he wasn't there. His new address was Churchill House. Wasn't that too, too grand! Exclamation marks marched across the page.

Poppy was reading the letter in Ben's bedroom, her room now. She had put up a poster of Adele to prove it, but it didn't look very convincing among all the cars and cricketers. Downstairs, Rico was teaching Jude to play chess. He'd offered to show Poppy too, but Jude had made it obvious she didn't fancy sharing her big brother. Jude was still cross, and Poppy thought it was a lot about jealousy and not liking having another girl in the house. The kinder Sally and Rico were, the crosser she got.

Poppy folded up the letter from Big Frank guiltily. She still hadn't told her mum about his move to open prison. Irena only talked about Poppy's grandpapa and his sadness and his need for her. Obviously she wanted to forget about her English family for the time being.

Homework would have to keep Poppy busy. School was the best place at the moment. The trouble was that tomorrow, Friday, the school was shut for a strike or teacher training or something and that meant Friday, Saturday, Sunday with bad-tempered Jude. If only she had somewhere to go! Will wasn't an option because he was going off with his mum – like other kids did, thought Poppy bitterly.

When her phone rang, she jumped on it with glee. 'Hello! Who is it?'

'It's Maggie.'

'Maggie?' Poppy had quite forgotten her.

'Sorry I didn't ring like I promised, but I heard Angel dropped in on you himself.'

Of course! Maggie was the lady who'd been kind to her when Angel was dancing about on top of the high-rise. 'Yes, he came over. Two days ago. He said he was in care.'

'With a family. That's right. An elderly couple. Not for long, I hope, for his sake. But I hear his mum's still in hospital.'

Poppy remembered that Maggie always knew about everything. She probably knew that her mum was in Poland and her dad in prison – or rather, 'open prison'.

'Poor Angel.'

'You should visit him.'

'Can I?'

'You're his friend, aren't you?'

'Oh, yes.'

'Well, then.'

After Maggie rang off, Poppy looked at the address she'd been given. In a nice road, Maggie had said, and not too far away. It would give her somewhere to go tomorrow – if she could slip away from Jude and her mum, that is.

The next morning, breakfast was late because there was no reason to get up early. It was raining again, rain dribbling down the window panes and plopping into the window boxes that Jude's mum had planted with bright red flowers.

'Morning, Poppy.' Sally looked up from her toast. 'Any sign of Jude?'

Poppy shook her head.

'I've booked a haircut for her this morning.' She looked at Poppy doubtfully. 'I don't expect you want one?'

She didn't expect absolutely right. Particularly as it was raining. In the rain Poppy's hair first looked like five hundred rats' tails, then stood on end like it had been scared out its wits.

'No thank you, Sally,' she said politely. Here was her chance to go and see Angel.

By the time Poppy found her way to the right house in the right street, her hair was dripping all over her coat and her coat was dripping all over her feet. She knew it was the right house because the door was painted black, surely a bad omen. No pretty window boxes here, although everything was very clean and tidy. If only she dared ring the doorbell!

Suddenly, the door burst open and a figure sprang out, shouting over his shoulder, 'Yeah! Yeah! Yeah!'

'Angel,' murmured Poppy, fearing she'd be overlooked as he rushed past her. She might have been a beetle. 'Angel,' she repeated louder.

He swung round, a bag swinging with him. Clearly, his arm was much better. No sling anyway.

'Hi. How do you know where I live?'

'You don't sound very pleased to see me.'

'I'm going out, aren't I.' Angel made an effort to slow down. Poppy puffed after him.

'Maggie told me where you lived. She told me I could visit you.'

'I don't know Maggie, do I.' He stopped abruptly and faced Poppy. Usually so cool, now his face was filled with urgency. 'She's wrong, your Maggie. I don't live there.'

Poppy stared helplessly. 'So where do you live?' As she spoke, she felt the rain trickle inside her coat and target her warm skin. She shivered. Things weren't going too well. But then, as Jude would say, nothing went well around Angel. He was still standing there, apparently immune to the rain, or perhaps it didn't get through his thick hair.

'I'm running away,' said Angel in his casual way, although Poppy could see he was serious.

'Really, running away for ever? Or just for the day?'

'Are you stupid, man?' Angel began walking again.

'Where are you running to?'

'Away, didn't I say.' He was now walking very fast.

'That's from, not to,' panted Poppy. She clutched at his arm to show him.

'Ouch!'

'Sorry.' They both stopped and looked at each other. Poppy shook her head so that wet drops flew off her hair as if she were a shaggy dog. 'I wouldn't mind running away.'

'I hadn't noticed it was raining,' said Angel, apparently mesmerised by the water whizzing about. 'Hey, if we're both running away, we'd better move further from the house before Bob takes a break from the TV and sees that bad boy's gone.'

Poppy followed Angel obediently. He always had that effect on her – made her want to follow.

They didn't talk for a bit, and soon the rain stopped and the sun came out, making the wet pavements steam. Poppy felt her hair drying and as it grew lighter, it rose up in the air.

'Where are we going now?' she asked.

'I need to say goodbye to the kids.'

'Seraphina and Gabriel?'

'Yeah. If that cow Eloise will let me.'

'Perhaps your mum's had her baby,' suggested Poppy hopefully.

Angel didn't answer this. He turned to her. 'Wow! That's some big hair you've got!'

Poppy frowned. 'No need to be rude.'

'I wasn't being rude, man. It's out of this world!'

To her amazement, Poppy realised he was actually expressing admiration. She thought of Jude sitting in the hairdresser having her neat straight hair made even neater, and smiled.

They reached the estate and looked up at the tall building clad in scaffolding with its lift stationary at one side.

Angel pulled up his hood. 'Don't need to be recognised.'

'...As the brave hero!' exclaimed Poppy, smiling. The morning was beginning to feel like an adventure, just the way things always did with Angel.

'That's where the hero slept.' Angel pointed to a battered armchair which was as wet as a sponge. 'Hero plus a family of mice,' he added, grinning.

'All drowned now,' said Poppy.

They carried on to the furthest tower block. Only then did Angel's high spirits begin to dim a bit. 'Saw my mum carried out,' he muttered, 'with that

Eloise woman shouting that she was dying. Gabriel bawling. Bad scene.'

Since Poppy could think of nothing cheering to say – it really did sound like a bad scene – they carried on.

'Up here.' Angel led the way up a dark concrete stairway. Black stains, possibly water, possibly something nastier, were slashed across the walls.

They took a lift up which smelled strongly of wee, until they reached the twenty-fifth floor.

'Nothing to a sky-walker like you,' said Poppy as they emerged, blinking in the brightness, on an open concrete walkway.

'Yeah.' Clearly Angel was nervous at the reception he might receive from his aunt. So was Poppy, if it came to that.

'Are you allowed to visit them?'

Angel shot her a black look. 'My own bro and sis?' Which didn't answer Poppy's question.

They continued along, and when Poppy dared a quick look over the parapet to the world below it made her feel all wobbly inside, even if they were a mere fifteen floors up.

Eventually they stood in front of a battered brown door, as if someone had forgotten their key and tried to break their way in. Inside, they could hear a small child crying.

'Gabriel,' said Angel. As if the sound spurred him on, he rang the bell then banged with his fists. Poppy doubted that it was the best way to introduce himself.

The door opened.

'You!' announced a woman who would have been like Angel's mum except that her face looked as if it had been blown up with a pump and she was about a foot taller and a foot wider, particularly on top. She was staring down at her nephew with as much horror as if a rat had knocked at her door.

'Yeah,' answered Angel bravely. 'Come to see the kids.'

'Ange! Ange! Ange!' A small figure hurtled through Eloise's legs and flung himself at Angel. Before his aunt could stop him, Angel picked up his brother and swung him in the air.

'Yeah! Yeah! Yeah!' shrieked the little boy delightedly. 'Ange gone.'

'Now I'm here. See Gabe,' and he threw him in the air again.

'And who is this lady with the sticky-up hair?' Eloise suddenly turned her attention to Poppy, who drew back nervously.

'I'm Angel's friend,' she said from a safe distance. Eloise's hands were the size of boxing gloves.

'Phu!' she commented dismissively.

'Where's Seraphina?' asked Angel, as Gabriel jigged up and down in his arms.

'You cannot be here.' Eloise took up a magisterial stance with her arms folded across her massive bosom. 'The Services have said you must stay away.'

'I want to see Sera,' said Angel obstinately. 'That's all. Be sure I'm not staying.'

To confirm this, Poppy nearly added, 'He's running away,' but decided not to draw attention to herself.

Then Gabriel piped up, 'Fina gone. Ange gone. Fina gone.'

'What does he mean?' Angel looked over his brother's head to Eloise. 'Where's Seraphina?'

Eloise reacted by snatching Gabriel from Angel's arms and blustering in a loud stream of unlinked words, 'Gone? Phu! Stupid, aren't you. Tell me something! Fine sister. What now. Go to the music. All work!' She ended with a final almighty 'PHU!' before rushing back into the flat and slamming the door.

Angel sprang forward and began ringing and

hammering again, muttering angrily as he did so, 'What has she done with Sera?' Then he began shouting, 'Seraphina! Seraphina!'

This had one effect. Several doors opened along the corridor and three women and one man emerged, all in a state of rage or at the very least, annoyance.

'What's going on?' mumbled a tousled-looking man dressed only in shorts.

'It's my sister,' said Angel wildly.

A woman with a baby looked more understanding. 'It's your Seraphina, is it? She told me she was going to look for you and her mum. She thought you were together, didn't she?'

'What do you mean? Where did you see her?" Angel rushed up to the woman, who was not much bigger than him.

'Don't be like that.' The woman stepped half-back into her flat. 'She was on the grass. I had a doctor's appointment, didn't I.'

'You mean she was ON HER OWN?' yelled Angel.

'Doctors don't wait, do they?' said the woman defensively.

But Angel had turned back to the door. 'Eloise, you fat old cow, let me in or I'll break the door down.'

After a few moments of this, Poppy suddenly saw Angel disappear forwards, and realised the door had been opened. She followed gingerly.

Chapter Fifteen

Poppy and Angel perched on a red-striped sofa, Gabriel between them. Eloise sat opposite them, her huge knees shining in tight black lycra. Her expression, however, was not shining. Not at all. It was black, like her tights.

'So you've lost Seraphina,' said Angel.

'Fina gone,' said Gabriel sadly, before giving a huge trusting smile to Angel.

It was a really pretty room, Poppy thought. Not what she'd been expecting at all. There was a colourful carpet on the floor and the curtains were white and lacy with beads threaded into them. In one corner there was a mountain of toys, including a large yellow car. A long shelf held a row of photographs of grinning children. No books, however, unless you counted the magazines stacked against the wall.

'I haven't lost her,' said Eloise, but without much energy. 'She's lost herself. That girl!'

'She's four,' said Angel severely.

'You find her, then!' Eloise fired up again and pointed a fat finger decorated with green nail varnish at Angel. 'You! You! Boy!' She shook her head tragically so that her dangling earrings bounced about her cheeks. 'What I have done for your family! And now you yell at me.'

'My mum gave you a home,' said Angel, but Poppy could see he was too anxious to be angry.

'You find her,' repeated Eloise. 'You're her brother.'

Poppy looked at Angel. Where were his plans to run away now?

'You know where she hides,' continued Eloise. 'Little girls like secret places. You're here, so you find her. See this: I wash my hands.' And she rubbed her sausage fingers together.

Poppy sat up straighter. Surely something was being forgotten here? 'Shouldn't you get in touch with the police?' she asked.

Both Angel and Eloise turned the same shocked expression on Poppy. For the first time they looked as if they might be related. Even Gabriel put his finger in his mouth and opened his eyes wide.

'The police find missing people,' said Poppy defensively.

At first she got no answer. Then Angel muttered, 'You want me in trouble again?'

'It's not you who's in trouble, it's your sister…' Poppy began, but faltered to a stop as no one took any notice.

Angel stood up. 'I'm out of here. Poppy, you coming?'

She was hardly going to stay, was she. To Gabriel's sad cries of 'Ange gone. Fina gone,' they left the flat. Angel didn't speak, as they made their way to ground level. All the doors along the corridor that had popped open were now shut, as if the people behind them wanted to make it clear they weren't going to help.

'So what are we going to do?' asked Poppy, when they were outside in bright sunlight. She tried to imagine what it must be like to have a younger sister. When she'd met Seraphina in prison, she'd been a lively, confident little thing, though she could hardly talk then. That had been ages ago.

'I know a few places,' said Angel.

'Do you want me along?'

'You're here, aren't you.'

This was not exactly gracious, but Poppy decided to put it down to nerves. Angel had his hood up and head down, but he did look behind him to see if she was following.

'Eloise's right about one thing. Seraphina likes to hide. She makes what she calls "houses" in all kinds of weird places and plays happy families there. It drives Mum crazy.'

'You mean, maybe she's run away like you?'

'No, man. Just looking for me and Mum, like that lady said.'

'She wouldn't go to the hospital, would she? It's nowhere near here.' They were outside the estate now and Angel hesitated. He glanced at Poppy. 'She'd look for me first, so I could help her find Mum.'

'So where would she look?'

'You want to come with me?' Despite everything Angel seemed to be smiling a little.

Poppy frowned crossly. 'Stop messing around.'

'Once she followed me under the flyover. Right to Snake's place where me and the brothers met.'

'Oh.' Poppy now saw why Angel might think she wouldn't want to come with him. 'Seraphina would never go there on her own, would she? Crossing all those roads. Wouldn't someone pick her up?' Seeing Angel's face, she added hastily, 'In a good way, I mean. Look after her.' She paused. 'Take her to the police station.'

'You've got police on the brain. There's a whole world the police never get to hear about.'

Privately, Poppy thought there were a lot of things the police *should* get to hear about, but she followed Angel without saying a word.

It was different, walking under the motorway with Angel leading her. The noise and the semi-darkness was the same, of course, but he was so obviously at home looking around and not taking shortcuts that she didn't feel at all scared. She did turn her face away as they passed the riding stables, in case Miss Horribly-Pip (she couldn't remember her real name) recognised her. But then it struck her that the riding teacher was just the kind of person to notice a little girl wandering around without a grown-up.

I'll ask for Seraphina at the stables,' she suggested.

Angel shook his head impatiently. 'Let's go to Snake's place first.'

Poppy suspected he really believed that he'd find his sister there, and continued to follow him.

Soon they saw the high fence with its advertisement tower in the middle. Nobody was in sight but anyone could be behind it. Poppy wondered why Angel didn't call out for his sister; he was beginning to crouch in a kind of stalking position.

'Do you think Seraphina's there?' she whispered.

Angel didn't answer. He continued forward carefully with Poppy staying close.

They reached the closed gates, and still there was no one to be seen.

'Come for a visit?'

Both Angel and Poppy swung round. Snake must have been creeping up behind them. He stood there grinning, his long legs splayed and his hands stuck in the back pockets of his black jeans.

'Yeah.' Angel took up his own tough-man pose.

Poppy looked from one to the other and didn't like what she saw. Snake could easily have a knife in one of those pockets.

'I see you've brought your bodyguard,' Snake sneered.

Poppy wondered who was guarding who.

'Have you seen her?' asked Angel, fiercely.

'Who?' Snake was nonchalant. 'I can see a she in front of me. That she I have seen.'

'You know who I mean,' said Angel, taking a step forward and clenching his fists.

Since Snake was a foot taller, didn't have a bad arm and might have a knife, to Poppy this seemed a seriously wrong move. 'He means his sister

Seraphina,' she said quickly.

'Seraphina. Oh, what a pretty name,' said Snake mockingly. He leered at Poppy. 'I never thought you'd be back. So where are your friends, then?'

'You had something to tell me yesterday,' interrupted Angel. His voice was hoarse. It made him sound desperate.

Snake turned his attention back to Angel. 'You went, didn't you? Didn't want to know me.'

'If you've seen her, tell me now!'

'Or you'll make me, will you? Aren't we brave in front of our pretty girlfriend!'

'She's not my girlfriend.' 'I'm not his girlfriend!' shouted Angel and Poppy at the same time. They both stared angrily at Snake.

Perhaps he'd got bored of teasing, because suddenly he put on an ingratiating smile and said in an oily voice, 'One brother to another.'

'Tell me,' repeated Angel, sounding even more furious.

'I was just having a quiet roll-up,' began Snake, giving Angel a smirk, 'when I heard a sweet little voice, singing out, "An-gel! An-gel! Where are you-u-u! An-gel". Then she stopped and began to cry a little. Wanting her mum, I expect.'

'Where was she?' asked Angel tensely.

'Here,' answered Snake. He stamped his foot on the ground. 'Right here.'

'Then what happened?'

'She saw me and ran away.'

Poppy reckoned that Snake was telling the truth. One sight of him, and anyone with any sense would run away.

'Did you follow her? Where did she go?'

'I called out her name – I'd seen her with you, bro – but she ran away fast, for someone so small.' He sounded admiring.

'You must have seen which way she went,' said Poppy.

'You.' Snake turned on Poppy. 'What business is it of yours!' He turned back to Angel. 'She ran towards the horses or the football.' He waved his hand vaguely. 'Over there somewhere.'

Poppy wondered whether to believe him, but Angel set off at once so she went after him anyway.

'Happy hunting!' came the horrible voice of Snake behind them.

'When did you and Snake talk?' Poppy asked when she caught up with Angel.

'Yesterday evening.' He stopped and faced her.

'Do you mean she's been out all night?' Poppy was horrified. 'In the rain?'

'No. No, I don't mean that. I think she headed home when she ran away from Snake. Even Eloise would have worried if she was away all night.'

'So she must have set out again this morning,' said Poppy.

'She's determined, that one.' Angel gave Poppy an appealing look.

Poppy wanted to suggest the police again. It seemed so obvious to her. They could look into all the nooks and crannies, hundreds of big men and kindly women on the job.

'What about your friend, Gus? He seems to know everything that goes on round here.'

Angel brightened. 'Yeah. Let's go.' Even so, he didn't hurry, as if it was worth a try but not much more.

It was just then that Poppy's mobile rang. 'Hi.'

'Poppy, is that you? I've been so worried.' It was Sally, Jude's mum. 'Where are you? You mustn't just go... '

'Sorry. I went for a walk.'

'In the rain? Where are you now?'

Poppy glanced at Angel. 'On my way back.

I'll be ten minutes.'

'Do you want me to pick you up in the car? I was worried. So was Jude.'

Not likely, thought Poppy. All the same, it was a nice feeling that someone cared about her. Angel was standing staring down at his feet. He looked very alone.

'Sorry,' said Poppy again. 'Don't bother about the car. It's not raining now. I'm fine.'

Sally rang off.

'I'll go find Gus,' muttered Angel.

'Yes,' agreed Poppy, turning away. It felt as if she was abandoning him.

Chapter Sixteen

Poppy had expected a grim reception when she got back to the house but nobody even mentioned her absence. Life had already moved on.

'Dad just rang!' cried Jude excitedly. He's taking the weekend off. He never takes a weekend off – it's his busiest time – but there's been a fire in the kitchen of his top restaurant where he's superchef. So he's decided we all need a holiday. We're going to a posh hotel in Wales run by a friend of his. Apparently there's a pool and all sorts of things to do.'

As Jude rambled on, Poppy couldn't help picturing Angel as she'd left him, alone, head down. But after a bit she got caught up in the planning of this special treat. How lucky to have two nights – they were going that afternoon – and two days out of London and in luxury!

Even when Jude revealed she'd invited Amber too, Poppy remained cheerful. Amber would keep Jude off her back and allow her to enjoy things her own way. After packing her clothes and a swimsuit, she added a book and then her diary. In the past that diary had always been her best friend.

Gus peered at Angel. The old man's bright blue eyes shone out of his lined, pixie-like face. Angel had found him in a dark little shed near the football ground. He'd been sitting at a table spread with sheets of paper covered in figures. He looked up with obvious relief when Angel put his head round the door.

'I hate accounts!'

'Yes,' agreed Angel, although he didn't know what accounts had to do with football. Then he told Gus about Seraphina.

'How old, did you say?'

'Four,' said Angel, and he heard just how bad that sounded.

Gus pushed back his chair and went to a shelf from which he took down two mugs, a carton of milk, two packets of sugar and a tin of cocoa.

Angel watched as he went to the corner of the dim shed and lit a small primus.

'Fire risk, I know. Don't tell anyone. But you've got to do things properly.' He measured out the milk into a saucepan and added the cocoa. He indicated a wooden spoon hanging nearby. 'Want to stir?'

Obediently Angel began to stir. He thought it was like a kind of ritual, a jungle magic man or something. Neither of them spoke as the milk gently simmered. Gus poured it into mugs and carefully added the sugar, stirring it with a spoon opened out from a penknife. These quiet actions made Angel feel calmer.

Gus sat down again and pulled over an up-ended box for Angel.

'So I can assume you haven't called the police?'

When Poppy had suggested the police, Angel had been irritated, but coming from Gus it seemed like something they could discuss.

'The police and me aren't too friendly.'

'Last seen stealing a ginger cake. I know.' Gus took a sip of his cocoa. 'What about your aunt?'

'She's brain-dead. Told me to find Sera myself.' Angel took a fierce gulp of his cocoa so that he burnt his mouth. 'Owwh!'

'Gently, son.' Gus gave a kindly smile. 'Your cards aren't too good, so it seems.'

Angel nodded. 'Bad scene.' He sipped his cocoa gingerly.

'So what are you going to do?'

Surprised, Angel looked up at him. Wasn't he going to tell him what to do? 'I don't know.'

'Where do you think she is?'

'Looking for me. I've been gone for a week. Then our mum went into hospital. She's still there.'

'I heard.' Gus took a last gulp of his cocoa and pushed away his mug.

Angel thought that his mouth must be as leathery as his face to be finished so quickly.

'Long practice,' said Gus, reading his mind. He grinned, making his skin wrinkle so close around his eyes that they nearly disappeared.

Angel found he was grinning too.

'That's better,' said Gus. He settled back in his chair. 'Two questions and two statements. Question one: do you want me to look after all this?'

'Yes,' answered Angel quickly.

Gus nodded. 'Question two. Do you think Snake's got your sister?'

This was harder. Angel realised that he half-wanted Snake to be guilty. But he knew deep down that even Snake would never do anything as bad at that.

'No-o.'

'No-o? Or no?' said Gus.

'No,' said Angel. 'But he did see her.'

'Good. I'll ask him. Statement one: I've changed my mind. You're going to start football training tomorrow. No contact. Just footwork. Any comment?'

'Cheers,' said Angel, smiling for the first time that day. 'What time?'

'Ten a.m. Don't be late. Statement two: I'm going to the police. Any comment?'

Gus looked at Angel and Angel looked at Gus.

'The police hate me.'

'Probably. Is it *you* that's missing? Excuse me, but I understood it was your sister.'

Angel blinked uneasily. It was him missing a few days ago, and it might be him again. 'They hate my whole family. My dad first, because he makes money in ways they don't like, so he's in and out of prison. Me, because they think I'm like him. My mum, because she can't sort it out. They just wish we'd all vanish in a puff of smoke. Why would they help us?'

'Because that's what they're paid for. It's their job. Believe me, son, I know what you're talking about. Years ago I was a bad boy: drugs – the more, the merrier. The police didn't like me and I didn't like them. I told you I was a boxer. Knew how to use my fists. But that's not the point. The point is, that despite their white shirts and epaulettes, big shoes and attitude, the feds are the best people to look for a four-year-old girl. Do you see that?' Gus looked hard at Angel.

Angel pictured Seraphina, her bright, knowing eyes, her fast zig-zagging run, the way she liked to climb over him when he was sitting down. 'The feds wouldn't want me involved?'

'They might need to question you.' Gus was still staring at him. 'But I'll go down to the station first of all with Eloise.'

'Eloise!'

'Unless you can locate your dad,' said Gus dryly. 'There has to be someone from the family.'

'Family!' Angel exclaimed disgustedly. He remembered why he'd got involved with Snake and the brothers. At the time they'd seemed like family. A lot of good they had done him!

There was a pause. The sun had come round and a bright shaft shone through the small window.

'I see you've got a bag with you,' said Gus.

Angel had forgotten all about his earlier plans.

'Going somewhere, are you?' continued Gus.

'Don't like those two dumb has-beens,' Angel was muttering, head down.

Gus laughed, 'I assume you're referring to Bob and Lee-Ann who, out of the goodness of their hearts, look after youngsters like you who are in a pickle.'

'They get paid, don't they?'

'True.' Gus stood up and peered out of the door of the shed, before turning back to Angel. 'Hang in there, Angel. That's my advice.' He thought for a moment, 'And maybe I'll see if I can persuade Lee-Ann to take you to see your mum.' He took a key from his pocket. 'Let's go. Me to Eloise and the station. You to drop your bag back in your room.'

They moved outside and Angel watched while Gus carefully locked the door. He glanced at Angel, 'Not that a wild one couldn't get in if he felt so inclined. Now and again my cocoa goes missing.' He walked over to Angel and gave him a high five. 'Cheers.'

'Cheers,' said Angel, and noticed that Gus was only a little taller than him.

'You haven't got a mobile, have you?'

'No.' Angel decided not to mention that his dad had pinched it.

'Here.' Gus pulled out a mobile, not new, not up to date, but still, a mobile. 'Keep that till tomorrow.

No calls to China, please. Now I'm off to find your sister!'

'Cheers,' repeated Angel to a fast-retreating back.

The sun sets in the west, Poppy told herself. That's why the sky ahead is red and orange. She was sitting in the back seat of a car driven by Jude's dad. He was so big and had so much dark hair, although she'd noticed a bald patch in the middle, that she had to peer through the side window to see out. Beside her Jude and Amber whispered together. But she didn't mind. She felt calm, pleased to be leaving London. In fact, she felt so calm that she closed her eyes and when she opened them again, they were in Wales.

'Wake up, we're in Wales!' Jude's face smiled at her in close-up, with Amber's an inch or two behind her.

'Whales?' Poppy murmured, still half-asleep.

'She thinks we're at sea.' Jude laughed delightedly and Amber joined in. Poppy woke up a bit more and thought it funny too.

Together they walked into the smartest hotel Poppy had ever seen. Even the bedroom the girls were sharing was big enough for several families.

'We'll have room service in our bedroom,' announced Sally, who'd come to fetch them. 'It's too late for the restaurant and Paolo' (her husband the superchef) 'wants to see what they'll send up.'

Poppy realised that they had entered a very different kind of world where everything was about enjoying yourself – even if it was a bit of business too for Jude's dad. She resolved not to think about any of her worries for the whole weekend.

Even so, she couldn't resist wondering about Angel as she lay in bed later. Had he found Seraphina? Then she reminded herself that he'd gone to get help from Gus, so that would be all right. She settled down comfortably.

The following morning, after a buffet breakfast in a beautiful yellow and white dining room – the waiter sliced fresh peaches to go with their cereal – the girls were led to a row of shining bicycles. 'Take your pick,' advised the man in charge, who was dressed in chic red cycling gear with the hotel logo on his jacket. 'I'm your host as we explore the countryside.' He was from Australia and very friendly.

This was just as well since Amber, who was ultra fit, wanted to race ahead up hills, while Jude was slower and Poppy slower still.

'I just feel lazy today,' she told Baz – his name was on his jacket.

'Don't worry.' Baz smiled at her with dazzling white teeth. 'I always bring up the rear and I like someone nice to talk to.'

'Is that you, Angel?'

Angel recognised Eloise's voice. He put the mobile closer to his ear, then sat down on the bottom stair. 'Yeah, it's me.' He was about to leave the house for his football date. Lee-Ann came out of the kitchen and looked at him enquiringly. She knew about Seraphina. In fact, most people did, now that the police were involved.

'Seraphina's back.'

Angel couldn't believe how Eloise was saying it as if it was nothing special. As if she'd found her glasses or something.

'She's back! How? When? Is she OK?' Angel saw Lee-Ann smiling and giving a thumbs-up. Lee-Ann wasn't so bad. Tomorrow afternoon she was taking him to see his mum.

'Two policemen and that Gus brought her back last night.'

'Last night? And you're only telling me now? That's low, man.'

'I'm telling you, aren't I. I've two kids in my care...'

'Care!' snorted Angel.

'If you want the truth, I wouldn't have told you at all without that Gus giving me your number and making me promise. I've enough troubles with your family. When do I want police in my living room eight o'clock at night?'

Angel held the phone further from his ear. Seraphina was back – that's what mattered. He'd ask Gus for details.

'Tell Seraphina I'll come round later,' he said, and quickly turned off the phone before Eloise could object.

The football ground was full of boys. Most of them wore either a white or a red bib. Angel approached warily. An older boy in a tracksuit jogged over to him.

'You the boy who went up the tower?'

'Yeah. Angel.' The boy looked all right, about seventeen, close-cropped hair, friendly.

'I'm Scope. Gus has made me your coach for the morning. Let's get ourselves something to kick.'

Angel followed him over to where Gus stood with a net of balls. Each one had a luminous G painted on it.

'They're a thieving lot,' commented Scope.

Angel thought how weird Gus looked with his white bristly hair and wrinkled, sunburnt skin. Like he was ninety. He was busy sorting out the teams and only noticed Angel as Scope was leading him off to a practice area.

'Hi, there, Angel boy. Wasn't that something with your sister. The whole force out looking for her and then she's found under the bed in your mum's room.'

Angel gawped. 'You mean, she was there when I went round?'

'Probably not. The kid's not clear. Seems to have gone and come back. She hid herself to escape the wrath of your aunt. Big hands, your aunt.'

Angel felt the good vibes of the morning drain

away. Had Eloise been thumping Seraphina?

'How did they find her?'

'Your kid brother brought her out to meet the police. Funny, that. You should have seen their faces. Your aunt's, too. Kid knew all along. Been giving her scraps of food.' Gus turned to a boy who had been trying to attract his attention by tugging on his arm. 'You're a winger, aren't you? So show me you can run.'

He turned back to Angel and said briskly, 'Off you go now. We'll talk later.'

Scope and Angel jogged over to the far end of the ground. Scope expertly dribbled the ball as he went. Angel watched enviously.

'Played a bit, have you?' Scope asked, when they arrived. Nearby, half a dozen boys were kicking balls into a net.

'Kicked around.'

'At school?'

Scope's eyes were mildly enquiring and Angel wondered whether to be honest, before deciding he'd probably heard worse. 'School and me didn't mix. Not much football the place I go now.' He gave the name, knowing Scope would recognise it as a school for excluded kids.

'There're one or two others from there.' Scope nodded. 'OK. Take it away up that edge.' As Angel set off with feet that felt as clumsy as tea trays, Scope shouted after him, 'And don't fall over. Gus says you have a stab wound in your arm!'

Thanks, thought Angel, as several boys looked up from their practising. Now everyone knows my problems.

In the afternoon, Poppy, Jude and Amber went to the hotel swimming pool. It was dressed up with palm trees and flowers and plastic parrots to look exotic.

'Welcome to the blue lagoon!' cried a woman in a sarong with a flower in her fair hair. 'I'm your hostess here today. I'm also a trained swimming teacher, so let's get started. How about a diving lesson?'

Beth, the name fixed on her swimming costume, also came from Australia. She had teeth just as white as Baz's and was just as kind and friendly. While sporty Amber showed off her diving skills, Beth swam beside Poppy and told her all about a pet koala she'd kept back home. Now and again, she interrupted herself to shout, 'Well done!'

to Amber as if she'd been watching, which she hadn't. Each time, she smiled conspiratorially at Poppy.

Jude was happy too. After a length or two, she'd taken her iPod to a turquoise-painted deckchair and lay there playing games. 'Soon Poppy joined her, leaving Beth to teach Amber how to do a somersault.

'I feel like a film star,' said Poppy dreamily. 'In Hollywood.'

Jude looked up from her game. 'It's fun, isn't it.'

Poppy sighed contently. 'Will the whole of the weekend be like this?'

'My dad likes organising things,' Jude said in a nice, not a boasting way.

'I feel so-o lucky!' Poppy stretched her arms over her head and it felt rather as if she was pushing away Angel, Big Frank and her mum too.

PART TWO

Chapter Seventeen

It's surprising how life goes on. The longer Poppy stayed with Jude's family, the more normal it seemed. No one took much notice of her – Ben was doing final revision for his exams and Sally had decided to try working now that her children were older, so instead of delicious smells coming from the kitchen, there were notes on the table saying, 'Food in fridge'.

Jude was no longer cross with Poppy, but made it clear that she preferred Amber's company. After school she and Amber did judo classes, swimming and gymnastics, none of which Poppy could afford.

This gave Poppy time on her own, which at first she didn't mind – or so she told herself. She talked to her mum every few days and she was beginning to sound more like herself. It seemed that Irena's aunt was planning to come and live with her papa, and then Irena could return to England.

One evening, Poppy told Irena about her dad's new prison. 'Soon he'll be able to come home for a weekend.'

'Oh! Oh!' her mum exclaimed, almost as if this was dreadful news. 'He will be on the streets, you say?'

'He can work outside the prison. After he's settled in.'

'Oh, my poor Frank! How will he manage?'

'But this is good news, Mum. You don't want him locked up for ever, do you?'

'No. How can you think! It is happy for him that he comes out. It is selfish of me that I like him to be safe and in no harm's way...' Her voice trailed away.

'Safe in prison, you mean? Safe behind high walls with barbed wire on the top?' Poppy was shocked. She thought of her dad, his big exuberant presence, his loud laugh, his red curly hair which he'd passed on to her.

'Of course he must be out. It is just the worry...' Again Irena left her sentence unfinished.

'Well, it's obviously harder for him if you're not here,' said Poppy sternly. 'When's your aunt coming?'

'Oh, that woman! She is not dependable. She pretends to be old, when in fact she is fifteen years younger than my dear papa.'

'It's not just Dad,' said Poppy. She was about

to complain about her own situation but stopped abruptly. Her dad was in prison while she was in a comfortable home. How could she compare the two? For months now she had succeeded in forgetting about him despite reading his letters. Now, all of a sudden, it felt as if he was her responsibility. 'Don't worry, Mum,' she finished lamely. 'We'll be all right.'

Immediately after this conversation, Poppy sat down and wrote to her dad, 'When can I come and see you? Are you allowed outside yet?'

And he wrote back, 'Not yet. Come whenever you like. But who can bring you, darling Pops?'

That was the problem. Poppy would need an adult to go with her to the prison. Jude's mum was the obvious person, but she was busy and Poppy already felt so embarrassed at overstaying her welcome that she hated asking yet another favour.

There was Will's mum, the GP, but she was busy too and Will said she was trying to find a place for them to live outside London. It hardly seemed the moment to ask her.

Then, in the middle of the night, Poppy woke up picturing Maggie – kind Maggie with the voluminous handbag and hundreds of children and grandchildren who'd looked after her when Angel had taken himself up to the top of the tower block. She hadn't seen Angel for ages – their lives were just so different – but that needn't stop her going to his estate.

The next day, Jude and Amber went one way to their judo class and Poppy went the other, to the estate. That was all she knew about Maggie – she lived on the estate.

It was a bright windy day with white clouds like flowers in the sky. Poppy enjoyed being out on her own and on a mission. Big Frank deserved a visit. Staring upwards at the huge buildings, she was disorientated for a moment. Where was the one clad in scaffolding?

'Heh! You won't find me up there!'

'You always did spring up from nowhere.' Poppy turned round smiling. 'Just as if you were a real angel. I was wondering where your building had gone.'

'The building's there. It's the scaffolding that's gone. So how's things?'

'Good,' Poppy lied. 'You?'

'I'm home. Mum had a son, Raphael. Another angel, see.' Angel grinned. 'Mum's in. Eloise is out. Yeah!' He raised his arms in a victory salute.

'Nasty woman,' agreed Poppy.

'Luckily, she blew her cover when Seraphina kept running away and the fat cow didn't even realise she was hiding under the bed?'

'Under the bed!' exclaimed Poppy.

'Didn't you know? Oh, man, that Seraphina is a law to herself.' He stopped and looked at Poppy. 'A long time since we met. Better times for me. You here for a reason?'

Poppy blushed guiltily. Obviously Angel had assumed she was looking for him.

'I'm looking for Maggie,' she muttered.

'Maggie? Maggie the maggot? Muppet Maggie? Maggie on the Moon?'

'She's a woman. Lives here. But I don't know where. I want her to take me to see Dad in prison.'

'Got it,' said Angel cheerfully. 'Mum knows everybody. She'll tell you.' He pointed in the direction of his flat. 'You can kiss the baby angel.'

Poppy followed him. There was something different about Angel. His walk, for a start – not a slouch but square-shouldered, feet picked off the ground, springy. His way of talking was different as well – more direct, less muttering. He seemed broader, too, or perhaps that was just the square-shouldered thing.

'How's school?' she asked tentatively.

'Boring. How else.'

So that wasn't it. Perhaps it was being at home again with his mum. Home! Not something she knew much about.

The flat was as pretty as she remembered, but this time it wasn't spoiled by the bad-tempered Eloise. Instead, Angel's mum sat on the striped sofa feeding the lolling baby. Around her feet Seraphina had lined up a row of dolls, turning face down the ones she insisted were behaving badly, saying loudly, 'Bad girl!' Meanwhile, Gabriel ran cars over the other sofa with a great deal of revving and screeching of tyres.

'Sorry about the mess,' said Maria.

'It's lovely,' said Poppy, and really meant it.

After Poppy had admired Raphael, who refused to open his eyes even when Angel tickled his chin, she asked about Maggie.

'Big lady with a big heart and an even bigger handbag,' smiled Maria. 'The whole estate knows Maggie.'

'Telephone number?' asked Angel.

'Gus will know how to get hold of her.'

'Who's Gus?' asked Poppy.

Maria, who was laying down the sleeping Raphael

on the sofa, stared up, surprised. 'Gus runs the football club where Angel spends his time. Thought you'd know that.'

'We haven't met for a bit,' Poppy muttered. She did remember Gus now.

'I'm going round there right this minute,' said Angel. 'Want to come?'

'I haven't much time.'

'So we'll walk quickly.'

In fact, they ran or at least, jogged.

'Do we have to?' panted Poppy.

'Part of the training.'

'I'm not in training.'

'I can see that.' Angel grinned and slowed down to a walk.

Soon they were under the motorway (which looked almost ordinary to Poppy now) and through to the sports ground. Rows of boys were sidestepping or stretching or whirling their arms.

'Hi, Scope,' said Angel, as an older boy came up.

'You're in the red team,' he said briefly, before moving on.

'Scope's my personal trainer. He's got muscles like iron.'

'Phew!' exclaimed Poppy, trying to be polite.

'He told me I've got a natural left foot,' added Angel, pride winning over modesty.

'That's good,' responded Poppy, wondering what an unnatural left foot would be. Maybe a goat's or a horse's, although they're natural too, just a different sort of nature... 'What?' She'd missed something Angel had said.

'I said, Gus is over there. You'd better catch him before the game starts. Got to go.'

'Thanks.' Poppy watched Angel jog away. That's the difference. He needs to good at something. Football. He's so focused, it's changed his shape.

'Hi, girlie. Come to cheer on the Bad Boys team?' Gus came up to her smiling. That was the thing about having hair like hers – no one ever missed her in a crowd.

'Is the team really called Bad Boys?'

'Officially we're Western Rangers United, but someone whose job entails driving round too fast with a siren on the roof of the car called us Bad Boys once, and it stuck.'

'Do the bad boys mind?'

'You do ask a lot of questions for a little girl. No, they like it. Now, what can I do for you? Or we'll have a load of bad boys stampeding over us.'

Poppy only then realised they were standing in the middle of the football pitch. 'Sorry. Can you tell me where I can find Maggie? Maggie from the estate who everybody knows? With the big heart and the bigger handbag?' she added, remembering Maria's description.

Gus rubbed his hand over his bristly white hair. 'I remember you now. You were with Maggie the afternoon I stopped Angel flying off the tower. He wanted to fly down to you, you know.'

'I didn't ask him to,' said Poppy defensively.

'I should hope not' – Gus was smiling again – 'or they'd have you in prison as a murderer.'

'Prison's the reason I want Maggie,' began Poppy but at that moment there was a blast from a whistle and Gus shooed her away.

'The laundrette,' he shouted in front of a wave of red shirts. 'On the way back to the estate. She works there evenings.'

One of the red shirts waved in Poppy's direction and she realised it was Angel, before he lowered his head, shot out his left foot and sent a ball flying to the other end of the pitch.

'A natural left foot,' remembered Poppy, smiling.

The laundrette was easy enough to find, not least because Maggie was standing at the door fanning herself with what looked like a folded pillow case.

Poppy felt suddenly shy, but knew that if she waited too long, she'd never dare approach her.

'It's me, Maggie.'

'It's you, is it, love? You-with-the-hair. Nice to see you-with-the-name-I-can't-remember.'

'Poppy,' said Poppy.

Maggie put away her fan, 'Just passing by, are you?'

'Not exactly.'

'You'd better come in, then.' She put on some flip-flops which lay by her feet. 'Gets hot here at the end of the day.'

There was no one else in the laundrette but a huge pile of bed linen. 'I don't mind the washing, but it's the folding that's hard. Good at folding, are you?'

So Poppy found herself holding the end of one sheet, and then another.

'What is it you wanted, love? Apart from saving my back.'

'I want you to take me to prison!' Poppy blurted out.

'Prison! Prison?' Maggie put away the folded sheet

and sat down on a green plastic stool. She pulled up a blue one for Poppy. 'Prison, is it? Some school project, I'm guessing. The things these kids get up to. Never been near a prison myself. Nor, I may boast, have any of my children, or grandchildren, although they'd be a bit young' – she chuckled to herself – 'been to prison.'

'I just need an escort,' mumbled Poppy.

'An escort,' repeated Maggie. She leant down and pulled from beneath her the vast handbag Poppy remembered from before. She settled it on her lap as if for protection. 'What about your mum or dad?'

'My dad's in prison. That's why I'm going there.' Poppy began to examine a strand of her hair as if it was very important. Maggie was so proud of none of her family being in prison, what would she think of her now? Poppy didn't dare look up to see.

She heard the little grunt heavy women give when they sit down or get up, and then a warm hand on her shoulder. 'You mustn't worry, darling. All sorts happen to the nicest people. Your dad probably had a bit of bad luck.'

'Yes,' said Poppy, trying to sound convinced. 'He is in an *open* prison.'

'There you are,' said Maggie comfortably.

'Now, we'll get on with the sheets before my client comes in and makes a rumpus, and you can tell me all about it.'

So, as they folded one sheet after another, Poppy explained at length how she was an orphan at the moment and her friend's mum where she was living had just started work and was too busy...

'And you thought of me.' Maggie closed the last sheet and sat back on her chair.

'Yes,' agreed Poppy.

'Well, I suppose everyone should visit prison once in their life...' Maggie's bag was back on her lap.

'Open prison,' intervened Poppy.

'Yes. Yes. Count me in, dear.'

Chapter Eighteen

Of course, nothing happened quickly.

Angel explained it to Poppy. 'Your dad will have to register Maggie as the adult, which means you need her full name and address.'

'Not just the laundrette, then,' said Poppy. She had got in the habit of going to watch Angel play football when Jude and Amber went off to their classes. Sometimes Will came with her but he had to hide it from his mum, who disapproved for no reason they could understand. Perhaps it was the 'bad boy' image of the players.

When Poppy sympathised with him about it, saying cheerfully, 'No one seems to care what I do,' Will turned on her fiercely: 'I hate all ball games anyway.' Even though Poppy knew this was because he'd never been well enough to play games, it didn't sound very friendly. She guessed he was jealous of Angel.

Angel really was very good at football. It wasn't

just his left foot: it was as if the whole of him became well-balanced and confident as soon as he got on to the pitch. Once Gus was standing near her watching Angel. 'Fast, strong and good with a ball. Just needs to learn to think.' He seemed to be talking to himself, so Poppy didn't defend Angel. She knew he could think. Not good at school, true, but very understanding. And you had to think to be understanding.

***

At last a date was set for Poppy's prison visit. She told Jude about it.

'You haven't seen him for ages, have you?' Jude sounded only mildly interested. She certainly wasn't begging to come too.

They were walking home from school together, one of the few things they still shared now and again.

'He's moved to a prison nearer London. In a few weeks he'll be allowed out to work, then he'll have weekends at home.'

'What? Without your mum?' Jude swung her bag so that it nearly hit Poppy.

'Mum will be back any time now,' Poppy said with a confidence she didn't feel.

Jude said nothing, making it clear she didn't believe a word of it. Poppy couldn't really blame her. She'd stayed far longer than expected. Soon it would be half-term.

'Who's taking you?' asked Jude suddenly.

'Maggie from the laundrette,' answered Poppy.

'Maggie from the laundrette?' Jude stopped and stared at her. 'I was just going to say that Mum would never take you – she wasn't very keen when I came with you all that time ago – but I can't see her letting Maggie-from-the-laundrette take you either.'

'She's very kind. She knows Angel...' Poppy stopped, at Jude's expression.

'That's a good thing? Knowing Angel?' Jude's voice was scornful.

'Angel's fine. He's part of this club,' began Poppy hotly.

'Football. I know.' Jude sounded bored and began to walk again. 'Anyway,' she said over her shoulder, 'If you want permission to visit the prison, I wouldn't tell Mum you're going with Maggie-from-the-laundrette.' She used a silly, mocking voice.

Poppy was cross. But later she thought that Jude had given her good advice.

Walking to the football ground the next day with Angel, she told him the problem. 'If Jude's mum thought Maggie was a teacher, it would be fine. Grown-ups think anyone who works at a school is reliable.'

Angel, who'd been doing little dancing steps and jabs in the air like a boxer, turned to face Poppy, still jabbing. 'Maggie did work at your school, didn't she?' Jab.

'Did she? I didn't notice her.'

'Dinner lady. Not very noticeable behind the hatch.' Jab. Jab.

'Maggie would be noticeable anywhere.'

'I don't know why you're arguing, man.' Angel began to do high skips. 'Just say she's from the school. Keep it brief.' He lunged forwards. 'You know, Gus says I could have been a boxer if I wasn't going to be a footballer.'

Poppy took Angel's advice, and Jude's mum said, 'Fine. Which Saturday?' without asking any more questions. Poppy suspected she felt a bit guilty about not going along herself. She did add, 'You've told your mum, I hope?'

'Yes,' answered Poppy, which was true enough. When she'd told Irena, her mum had cried out, 'Oh. Oh. Oh. I must come back to your papa!'

But she hadn't, and that was two weeks ago. So Poppy was the only one trying to help Big Frank.

She asked Angel whether he thought her mum was having a breakdown, hoping he'd say something reassuring. 'Probably,' he answered laconically. 'They get more and more stressed out, these so-called grown-ups, and then they go POP!' He jumped in the air.

'Thanks for that,' said Poppy.

'I expect she prefers to go POP' – he jumped again – 'in Poland, where she grew up.'

'You may be sportsman of the year,' said Poppy crossly, 'but you could keep still occasionally.'

'Sorry.' Angel lay down at her feet.

Actually, Poppy thought he was right. Irena was recovering from the difficulties of life in London at her childhood home in Poland, with the excuse of looking after her papa. Which left Poppy in charge of her own dad. Funny, how grown-ups always make things more complicated than they are.

⁂

It was raining slightly when Poppy and Maggie met for their visit to the prison. Maggie, who'd decided to pick Poppy up, stood outside the house in a transparent purple mackintosh.

'Who's that weird woman?' asked Jude, peering through the window.

'That's Maggie,' said Poppy. She did look rather weird, mainly because she was holding her huge bag under her mac.

'You never told me she was *deformed*,' said Jude.

'She's not!' hissed Poppy. 'It's her bag!' She opened the door.

'Morning, love.' Maggie smiled with her usual warmth. 'Not the best day for an outing. But I suppose we won't see much of it where we're going.' She lowered her voice and whispered loudly, letter by letter, 'P-R-I-S-O-N.'

'Bye, Jude.' Poppy hurried out of the door. 'Tell your mum I've gone with Maggie,' she added over her shoulder.

'I certainly will.' Jude shut the door firmly.

Poppy and Maggie proceeded to the underground. Once they were inside, Maggie extracted her bag from under her coat and handed it to Poppy, 'Be a dear and hold it a moment. Plastic's much too hot for going through tunnels.'

Poppy watched as she shed her coat the way a snake sheds his skin – starting at the top and stepping out of it at the bottom. Maggie stood for a moment as if expecting admiration.

Poppy stared, and was lost for words. Maggie was clad from head to toe in orange, blue and pink stripes. She looked more like a deck-chair than a human being.

Since Poppy was speechless, Maggie filled the gap happily. 'I thought the poor dear men locked up in cells would be cheered by a bit of colour.'

'I'm sure they will,' Poppy managed to say at last, and they went towards the barrier. As they settled on the train, Maggie dug out a Kit Kat for each of them from her bag. Poppy tried to imagine what her dad would make of Maggie, and failed. Then she told herself it didn't matter. Maggie was kind; that's what mattered. Even more important, she was sitting beside her, taking her to see Big Frank. Who else was going to do that?

Less than an hour later, Poppy and Maggie got off the train at a station in the middle of the nowhere.

'So where's the prison, then?' It was still raining and Maggie had put her transparent mac back on, but now she seemed to have shrunk inside it.

A cow mooed somewhere and they both jumped. 'We'll ask,' said Poppy.

'I don't like the idea of prisons at all,' grumbled Maggie as they walked towards the exit.

'My dad did do something wrong,' Poppy pointed out.

Maggie ignored her. 'As if treating people like wild animals ever helped anything.'

'Maybe an open prison's different,' said Poppy.

The station forecourt was completely deserted apart from parked cars and a minibus about to depart.

'Excuse me!' shouted Poppy, feeling someone had to be leader and it wasn't going to be Maggie.

The driver peered out. 'Lost, are you?'

'We know where we are...' began Poppy.

The man, who had a broad friendly face, smiled. 'But?'

'...not where we're going. At least, we know where we want to go...'

'But not how to get there,' completed the driver. 'So where are you going?'

Poppy realised she was getting all tongue-twisted because she didn't want to use the word 'prison'. Suddenly inspired, she shouted, 'Churchill House!' Not like a prison at all.

'Ah,' said the man, 'That place. I happen to be driving there myself. May I offer you a lift?'

At the word 'lift', Maggie who'd been staring blankly ahead as if the conversation wasn't happening, came to life.

'Sir, you are a true gentleman.' She walked firmly towards the bus and looked over at the driver, who had begun to grin again. 'I could tell that at once. But don't tell me you work in that godless place?'

'In a manner of speaking.' He put his hand through the window. 'I'm Bob. Hop in, and we'll have you there in style. Madam in the front with me and Miss in the back.'

Poppy introduced them – 'I'm Poppy and she's Maggie' – as they obeyed his command.

'You're lucky to have hit on me,' began Bob chattily as they set off, after he had extricated the gear lever from the handle of Maggie's bag. 'I was dropping off some of the lads for that train you came in on.'

'They get out, do they?' said Maggie, as if she didn't really believe it.

'I told you they work,' said Poppy.

'Yes, indeed,' said Bob, who was negotiating the country lanes at speed. 'They're working inside a freezer today. Cleaning it. Minus forty degrees. Can't say I envy them, though the pay's good.' He stopped to let a gigantic red tractor turn across the road into a field. 'Of course, mine's the cushiest job. But then, not everyone at Churchill has a clean driving licence.'

Maggie and Poppy took this in. 'Do you mean, you live there?' asked Poppy tentatively.

'Nine months it's taken to get myself the cushiest job and the biggest room.'

'You're a prisoner?' exclaimed Maggie, rather as she might have said 'alien'.

'Not much longer,' Bob continued cheerily. 'Unless I go mad and attack the psychiatrist, I'm out in forty-one days.' Since Maggie didn't respond, he continued, 'So who are you visiting? I assume you're visiting.'

'My dad,' said Poppy quickly. 'Frank. Perhaps you know him?'

'Big chap with red curly hair?' Bob sounded less

enthusiastic.

'Yes. He's expecting us.'

'I expect he is.' Bob became silent and drove even faster.

After many more country lanes, so that to Poppy the whole world seemed a green blur of trees and hedges, the bus pulled up just inside a fence and gates.

'I'm not supposed to pick up passengers so I'll let you off here. Have a good day!'

Poppy and Maggie watched the minibus sweep off down the driveway. They felt very alone. At least it had stopped raining. Maggie slithered out of her mac again, folded it carefully and stowed it away in her bag.

'Here we go, love. Chin up. Your dad will be glad of a hug.' It seemed that she'd got her nerve back.

They proceeded briskly up the paved drive and eventually saw what looked like a large country house. To their left, a sign saying VISITORS pointed to a more modern building.

Poppy thought of the two other prisons where she'd visited her dad. She shut her eyes for a moment. But when she opened them again, there were still no high walls with barbed wire on the top, no noise of barking dogs – only the sound of wind in the trees. She followed the moving deckchair that was Maggie through a door, and found they were in a reception area. Once more, there was no obvious security.

'It's not usually like this in prison,' she explained to Maggie.

'More's the pity,' replied Maggie bracingly, before turning to the receptionist whose prison officer uniform came as a bit of a surprise, 'We've come to see her dad, Frank. He's expecting us.'

The woman, who was young with pink lipstick, looked at Poppy. 'You've brought out the sunshine, haven't you, dear.' She nodded at Maggie. 'We've got a lovely garden for the kids. Budgies and bunnies. All kinds of fun.'

'I've come to see my dad,' said Poppy, not liking her patronising tone.

'Oh, the men can go out too. I sometimes think they like the animals more than their own kids. Not that I'm saying your dad's like that... Just go straight in and I'll tell him you're here.' She pointed to a door.

'Don't we have to lock our things away?' asked Poppy.

'Oh, no, dear. Although the men do when they come back from work – hand over their mobiles, that sort of thing. Off you go now.'

The visiting room was a bit more like a prison with two officers lounging against the wall and several families already there.

'We'll have this table,' said Maggie, leading the way. 'Furthest from them' – she indicated the officers.

Poppy decided that Maggie was trying to create a bit of drama. The prospect of seeing Big Frank after such a long time was quite enough excitement for her. She sat down warily.

'Pops. Darling Poppy. So here you are!' He had approached silently from behind. He held out his arms and Poppy leapt up and flung herself into them.

'Oh, Dad! I can't believe it's really you!' So she wasn't an orphan after all. Here was Big Frank, smiling face, broad chest, solidly on his feet to give her the first proper hug she'd had for years – well, it felt like years.

'You've grown ten inches,' said Frank, as he put her down,' and your hair another ten.' He looked at Maggie, who was sitting demurely upright with her vast handbag clasped on her lap. 'And who is this lovely lady?'

'It's Maggie.'

'It's Maggie, is it? Well, I'm pleased to meet you,

Maggie. You're a kind lady to escort my Poppy when her mama is over the sea and far away.' He raised his arm as if to shake hands, then changed his mind. 'How about a nice cup of tea?'

'I wouldn't say no.'

Frank smiled. 'You'll be the one buying it.'

'I'll do it!' Poppy offered eagerly. But first of all Maggie had to unearth her purse from her bag. Poppy and her dad watched, amazed, as a bottle of scent, a pencil case, a make-up bag, a fluffy hat, two mobiles, a pair of socks, a ball of wool and a stuffed monkey were pulled out and laid aside. At last the purse appeared.

'Eureka!' cried Big Frank, and Maggie gave him a suspicious look.

When Poppy came back with two teas and a Coke on a pretty round tray, Big Frank was still standing up. She noticed a change in him: he was fatter, paler and seemed on edge, more like when he'd first gone into prison.

'Do you sleep in that nice big house we saw?' she asked him, since no one else was speaking.

'Nice, my—' He stopped before saying a bad word and looked down at her bitterly. 'A hundred years ago, it was the kind of orphanage where they prepared poor kids to go off and be slaves in Australia. Now they've carved up the inside so it's a warren of corridors and bedrooms, some of them fit for a king, some for a corpse.'

'I hope you have a big one, being so big yourself,' said Poppy politely.

'It's a coffin,' answered her dad briefly. Still standing, he gulped his tea before putting down the cup on the table with a clatter.

He is so restless, Poppy thought. Surely he should be happier now he's in an open prison.

'I'll be working next week,' he said abruptly. 'Cleaning trains. Those people you see scurrying about before you get on. Plastic gloves, plastic bags, that sort of thing.'

For the first time, Maggie showed signs of wanting to join in the conversation. She shifted her bag to the floor and leant forward confidentially, 'Trains are dirty by nature. You'll never get a train clean.'

Poppy looked at her dad. It seemed a pity to depress him about his fresh start in the world outside. Anything can be cleaned, surely. But he hardly seemed to be listening.

'It's being near people going out each day, going home, seeing their wives, kids…' He seemed to be talking to himself and began pacing backwards and forwards, two steps one way, two steps the other.

'That's going to be you, Dad!' Poppy cried.

He stopped, and gave her a smile so that he almost seemed normal again, before reverting once more to his gloomy restlessness. 'If I don't get sent back. They've got their eye on me. I couldn't bear that, Poppy.'

Suddenly he sat down and took her hands. 'Anything I do is for you, Poppy.' His voice was filled with love and pain. 'It almost feels like I've lost your mum, already. But you, Poppy, you'll never desert me, will you?'

Frightened by his tone, Poppy cried out passionately, 'Of course I won't, Dad! But why are you talking like this? Mum will be back soon, and you're in an open prison. What's wrong! I don't understand.'

'No, no. How could you?' He withdrew his hands and dropped his voice so that Poppy could hardly hear. 'There're temptations here. Work of the devil, no doubt. Call them temptations or possibilities. What future is there for me if I come out of here with no money, no job, no wife maybe...?'

'Mum will never leave you!' cried Poppy. 'It's just that Grandpapa needs looking after.'

'Yes. Yes. I expect you're right.' He sounded impatient, as if she'd interrupted his train of thought. 'It's too good to miss, that's the truth of it. Work for a week so nobody gets anxious, then go for it.' He was talking to himself again. 'Devil wins but takes us all with him. I'd be a crass idiot to turn them down...'

'Dad! Dad!' Poppy tried to get his attention. 'What is it? Are you planning something? Is it dangerous? Is it wrong? Dad, tell me!'

Big Frank looked at her unseeing for a moment, then abruptly his attitude changed and he became an affable dad once more, delighted to be with his daughter. 'What do you say we go out to the garden! I hear they have a whole aviary out there – cockatoos, peacocks, you name it...'

For the rest of the visit, he was jolly as could be. He asked Poppy all about school, then began to imitate Mr Hannigan, the headmaster, fingers tapping an imaginary desk, starting each long-winded sentence with 'Ah, indeed, now...' just the way the headmaster did. Poppy was in fits of giggles and Maggie was laughing so much, she had to get a handkerchief out of her bag to wipe her eyes, which was another performance.

Then he started on Maggie, flirting outrageously,

'My dear madam, may I say how much I admire your choice of clothing. On a dull day, it would light up all around. As the sun is now shining' – he swept his hand up to a clear blue sky – 'you are in tune with the wonders of nature. In fact, you are a natural wonder.' Here he dropped to one knee. 'And as such, may I kiss your hand or – if you withhold that – your dainty foot!' And he bent down over Maggie's large turquoise sandal. Once again, Maggie's hankie had to be searched for in the bag.

When they eventually left, walking out to a cab ordered by reception, Maggie squeezed Poppy's arm. 'You never told me your dad was such an entertainer!'

'Oh, yes,' said Poppy. 'He used to make all my friends laugh when he picked me up from school.' But even as she spoke, she remembered his strange whispered words. Maggie hadn't heard, so there was no point in talking to her about it.

Poppy got in the cab and sat quietly. She was quite sure Big Frank was planning to do something desperate. But how could she know what? And how could she stop it?

Chapter Nineteen

Angel looked at Poppy seriously. She had just told him about her visit to Churchill House and the strange things her dad had said. Angel was wearing football boots and every now and again he aimed a kick at an orange cone.

'It sounds to me as if your dad's gone POP now.' He gave a ferocious lunge. 'He's planning to blow everything and do a runner.'

'But he can't!' wailed Poppy.

'Nothing easier. You say he's cleaning trains. He gets on with his bag at the start of the day and doesn't get off. Could go to France if he liked. Nobody will know he's gone for eight hours.'

'I don't mean that sort of can't. Of course he can. He's trusted. In an open prison. Even I understand that. What I mean is, if he does do a runner, he's sure to be caught and then he'll be back in that horrible prison on that island. And he'll be gone for ever! Why would he risk that?' Poppy felt like crying.

'Yeah. Strange choice. Very few mess up right at the end. Funny, isn't it? When he first went in you wanted to help him escape, and now you want to help him to stay in.'

'That's when I didn't know he was guilty. Anyway, I'm not interested in whether it's funny.' Poppy shook her head crossly.

'I see that, man.' Angel looked down thoughtfully. 'He must think he can get something really big out of it, to take the risk. Only crazies run from an open prison.'

'We've got to stop him!'

'Yeah. Like we don't even know what day he's planning on skipping. Or where he's heading.' Angel gave a small kick, before restraining himself. 'He'll have a mobile when he's outside. Maybe you can get something out of him if you call him. If he's all restless like you say, it's worth a throw. He might need to talk to someone.'

'An-gel!' a voice called from across the pitch.

'Got to go. Try that call. I'm in to help, man. Be cool.'

Waving a hand, Angel ran off.

Poppy walked away slowly. She'd call her dad next week. But it seemed a long shot.

⁂

'It's *me*, Dad!'

'Who? Who is it?' Poppy was shouting, but her dad didn't seem able to hear her.

'It's me. Poppy!' Now she was yelling.

'Wait for the station announcement to be over.' So that was the noise in the background. He must be doing his train-cleaning job. There was a pause.

'I might be able to hear now. His voice was loud and clear. Who is it?'

'It's your daughter.'

'Poppy? Why didn't you say? How have you got my number?'

'You gave it to me when I came to see you. Don't you remember?'

'Did I? I'm working now. Can't talk.'

'I want to come and visit you again. This Saturday.'

'Saturday! But you've only just been!' He sounded so shocked that Poppy immediately suspected he didn't want her to visit him. Was that because he knew he wouldn't be there?

She decided to push him. 'It was a really easy journey, and Maggie loved the countryside.

She wants to come again.'

'I told you, I can't talk.' Poppy could hear another station announcement in the background. 'I'll ring you tonight.'

'OK,' agreed Poppy, but the line was already dead.

That evening, Poppy pretended she had extra homework and went to her room immediately after tea. Instead of working, she lay on her bed with her mobile in her hand. It rang at seven.

'Yes, Dad!' she answered immediately.

'It's me. Will. You sound odd.'

'I'm waiting for a call.'

'Let me guess. From your dad.'

'Clever.'

'I didn't know your dad ever rang you.'

Poppy took a breath. 'He's in an open prison.' She wondered whether to tell Will her worries. In the past he'd been part of all her plans to do with her dad. And she might need more than just Angel to help stop him running off. 'Look, Will, this is top secret.' Then she told him everything, ending, 'I'm trying to find out when he's going to do it so that we can stop him. Angel's on for it.'

'That's great!' exclaimed Will. 'I was feeling really bored.'

''This isn't a game to cheer you up, you know! This is serious,' Poppy said crossly.

'Sorry. Sorry. You're quite right.'

'OK. I'll let you know when I have more details.'

'I'm on standby.' Will rang off and Poppy decided he was a good friend, if a bit insensitive.

Her mobile rang again half an hour later. This time it *was* her dad.

'Hi, Poppy. Sorry about earlier. I was on a train with my bag and brush.' He gave a loud laugh. But there was something odd about the laugh. Not relaxed. Not like himself.

Poppy decided to test him. 'It must be great to be working.'

'Great to be collecting other people's rubbish and dirt. Yeah, really great!' His voice was horrid and jeering.

'But to be outside again. In the world. That must be amazing!'

'Allowed out. Like a naughty child.' His voice was slurry now.

'Dad! You'll be out soon! You'll be home!' Why couldn't he play by the rules?

'Hey, Pops. You'd like to be proud of your dad, wouldn't you?' Now his tone was wheedling. 'Have him rich and successful?'

'No!' Poppy cried out. 'I want you home.'

'Well, I'm not coming home like a poor, miserable, failed thing.' Suddenly he sounded furious. 'I'd rather not come home at all!'

'But Dad…' began Poppy, almost in tears.

'Don't "But Dad" me. You don't know what I've been through – the humiliations. And now it's almost worse. I'm a train-cleaner. Up before dawn. On the train by seven-thirty. Rubber gloves, stinking bits of food, sticky cans, bottles, tissues, nappies – this isn't a job for a man! I've still got a bit of pride left. And now I've got a real chance to make something of my life. Monday, Tuesday, Wednesday, I'm the lowest of the low, then Thursday I'm off. Train to Heathrow. Flight to Belfast. Pick up the stuff at Larne. Over the border. Hand it over. Take the money. Put it somewhere safe. Lie low for a few days. Turn myself in. Rich. Rich. Rich. RICH! It'll be worth another year or two in H.M.P. Castlerock.'

'Dad. Dad!' wailed Poppy. She realised he was

somewhere she couldn't reach him. It was like Angel said: he'd gone POP and entered a world where she was shut out.

Now she could hear his heavy breathing. She didn't know whether to ring off or not. But at least she knew what he was planning, and when.

Thursday. A school day.

'Dad?' She said gently after a minute or two.

His breath slowed and became softer. 'Hey, Pops. Sorry I went off like that.' His voice sounded normal again. 'Sometimes it just gets to me. I can't even remember what I said just then. Whatever it was, don't take too much notice. We prisoners do a lot of imagining in our cells.'

She wanted to believe him. But his plans had sounded too concrete: Belfast, Larne, the stuff – she could imagine what that was – hiding it and then, when everything was quiet, turning himself in. It was all too detailed, too real.

'I really would like to come and see you, Dad.'

'Leave it. Just leave it!' His voice was hard again.

'OK,' said Poppy hastily. 'I'm sure Mum will be back soon and then we can come together.'

He didn't comment. 'Bye, Pops. Darling Pops, remember, whatever I do is for you!'

As he rang off, Poppy thought that wasn't much consolation. In fact, it made her feel worse if she was the reason he was going to do wrong and dangerous things. Of course, she knew that the true reason was his manly pride and his longing to be 'rich, rich, RICH'. But that wasn't good either.

When Poppy had forgiven her dad for doing bad things and going to prison. she had never thought he would do something wrong again.

Poppy twirled a long red curl round her finger, then let it spring out again. The important thing was to stop him acting out his plan.

Poppy, Will and Angel met in Poppy's house She had told Jude she was going to pick up any mail.

They sat in the kitchen and Angel said, in a boasting kind of voice, 'Can't believe I lay under this table bleeding to death.'

'You weren't bleeding to death,' said Poppy, who was keen to get on to the subject of her dad.

'I was certainly out of my mind,' insisted Angel.

'You had been stabbed by your mate,' said Will kindly. 'Has it healed OK?'

'Better than new. You should see me in goal.'

'Oh, football.' Will sounded bored.

'We're not here to talk about Angel,' interrupted Poppy impatiently.

'Yeah. Yeah.' Angel tipped back in his chair and put his arms over his head. Poppy thought that all his confident sportsman attitudes were making him uncaring. Then he tipped his chair smartly forward again and said, 'So how are we going to catch Big Frank before he goes? He's sure to do it first thing, to give himself the maximum time before his disappearance is clocked.'

Will frowned intently. 'Best thing would be to catch him on the train to the airport.'

'That won't give us long,' said Poppy. 'And anyway, he might go by Tube.'

'You think it'd be easier at Heathrow? There might be a lot of early morning flights to Belfast.'

'Can we pinpoint the time?' asked Angel.

Poppy thought hard. 'When Dad was ranting, he said they're working on the trains by seven or seven-thirty in the morning.'

'So let's say he does his job for half an hour, then buys a ticket and skips straight on to the airport.' Will counted, 'Seven-thirty, eight, eight-thirty

Heathrow, nine-thirty flight.'

'That would give us an hour to find him,' said Angel.

'He's big, as you know,' said Poppy, 'and he's grown his hair again – my sort of hair.'

'Not easy to miss.' Will and Angel nodded seriously.

'I'll check all flights between nine and eleven,' suggested Will. 'I can do it on the computer when Mum's out.'

'Do you think three of us are enough?' Poppy had a dismal picture of them standing on the viewing platform and Big Frank waving to them as he took off in his plane. Just like when Jude and she had watched her mum leave. What a lot had happened since then!

'I suppose I could ask Jude,' she said doubtfully. 'But I haven't told her anything.'

'There's another problem,' said Will. 'We'll have to skip school.'

'You're always missing school,' Poppy pointed out. 'Just say you're ill.'

'What about you?'

'I don't care,' said Poppy bravely. 'I won't turn up, that's all. Some things are more important than school!'

Angel laughed loudly. 'Say that again.'

'OK. So let's get this clear.' Will had his organising voice on. 'We all leave for school as normal, then head for Paddington to catch the train to Heathrow.'

'How do you know it goes from Paddington?'

'Never heard of the Heathrow Express? Anyway, it's our nearest station. Meanwhile I'll check on flights.'

'How do you know all this stuff?' asked Angel, looking impressed.

'I've always had too much time.'

'No football,' said Angel.

'No football,' agreed Will.

Poppy was glad the two boys were getting to respect each other, but she still felt jittery about their plan.

'Maybe Dad's working at Paddington, she said.

Will smiled. 'Then we'll catch him even earlier.'

'Just threaten him with the police and he'll be back with his rubber gloves and cloth in a flash.' Angel smiled too.

That was the whole idea, of course, but Poppy still felt worried. What if Big Frank went POP again and did something stupid. Like, like… Her imagination failed.

'We'll need money for the train fare,' she said.

Will frowned unhappily. Clearly, money wasn't his strong suit. Nor was it Poppy's, if it came to that.

Angel, on the other hand, looked brightly at them, 'I've got money,' he said.

They stared at him.

'Yeah. Dad dropped by to see the new baby. Raphael. Nice of him. He slipped me a roll when Mum wasn't looking.'

'A roll?' queried Poppy.

'A roll of notes.' Angel grinned. 'All twenties. I counted. Fifty notes.'

'Phew,' said Will, doing the sum. 'A thousand pounds!'

'Don't ask where they come from,' Angel laughed.

'Isn't that called Receiving Stolen Goods?' asked Will stiffly.

'Can't be sure where they come from, can I?' Angel pushed back his chair and stood up. 'But if you don't want them, that's no problem.' He scowled at Will.

'Sshh, both of you.' Poppy tried to sound soothing but only succeeded in making an anxious gulping noise. 'It's my dad who's in trouble and if Angel's got the money we need, then I'm asking no questions. In fact, I'm saying a big thank you. And do sit down, Angel.'

'OK,' said Will a bit sulkily. 'Don't bring the whole thousand, though.'

'As if!' said Angel, but he did sit down.

The respect between them hadn't lasted long. They were just too different.

'So, we've got a basic plan.' This time Poppy tried to sound bossy. 'But do we want to involve more people?'

They all thought hard. 'Gus would be cool,' said Angel.

'Wouldn't he tell the police right away?' asked Poppy warily.

'No, man. Gus isn't a friend of the feds – except when he needs them. He's a busy guy. But I could ask.'

'Maggie might come, I suppose.' Poppy half-smiled at the thought of Maggie chasing Big Frank round the airport. 'She loves drama.' She paused, before adding, 'So does Jude.'

'Hey, how many bodies do we need here?' asked Will. 'Let's get the facts first – time of flights, which terminal – and then decide.'

'Fine by me. I should be off now, anyway.' Poppy stood up to go.

Chapter Twenty

Planning is one thing: action another.

It was Thursday morning, and Poppy opened her eyes so early that the blackbird that usually woke her with his cheeping was still asleep. She pulled the bedclothes over her head. What if everything went wrong and her dad got arrested? What if he got arrested before they got to him? What if he evaded them and flew off to Ireland? What if they all got arrested for what Will called 'aiding and abetting'? Then Angel would be put back into care. And perhaps she would too. Poppy tossed and turned.

Eventually she got up, dressed and went down to the kitchen.

'You're early,' said Jude's mum, sipping a mug of tea.

'You're early,' said Ben, looking up from his book.

'You're early,' said Jude, who was sleepily coming down in her pyjamas.

'I want to get to school early.' Poppy crossed

her fingers against such a whopping lie.

'I'll drop you off, if you like,' said Jude's mum.

'No, thanks. I'll be fine,' said Poppy hastily.

'I wouldn't mind getting in early today,' said Jude.

However much Poppy tried to put her off, Jude, who had shown no interest in her for ages, insisted on coming along with her.

They set off well before eight, with Poppy still racking her brains about how to escape. She needed to catch a bus to Paddington Station where she'd meet the others.

Suddenly she caught sight of Maggie – not easy to miss in Coca-Cola red with matching earrings.

'Oh, there's Maggie!' Poppy waved and shouted, 'Maggie! Maggie!'

Maggie heaved her bag from one arm to the other and waved too. 'Morning, love.'

Poppy turned to Jude, 'I've just got to tell Maggie something,' she said, as if it was urgent – well, actually it was. 'I'll see you in school.'

'But you said you wanted to be in early,' said Jude reasonably enough.

'I do. I do. I won't be long. You go ahead.'

Jude let her go – clearly she didn't fancy being

seen with Maggie.

'Quick! Quick!' said Poppy to Maggie, who was as bewildered as Jude. 'We've got to go round the corner so she can't see us.' She took hold of Maggie's voluminous sleeve and began to drag her along.

'That's all right, dear, I'm coming,' said Maggie kindly. 'Your friend seems a bit upset.'

'She'll get over it,' muttered Poppy, as a bus appeared in the distance. 'I've got to catch this bus.'

'Surely it's a school day, dear?'

'The thing is…' began Poppy, then stopped. How much dared she tell Maggie? They had considered including her in their plans. 'The thing is…' Just then she caught sight of Will lurking at the entrance to a shop near the bus stop.

'Yes, love.' Maggie smiled. 'Spit it out. I haven't been shocked since I was twelve and my dog dropped dead at my feet. On my feet!'

So Poppy told Maggie everything about Big Frank's decision, and how they were going to save him from himself because he wasn't really bad, just had bad ideas and anyway he was her dad. By the time she was describing their plan of action, they had reached Will, who stopped lurking and came to join them. There was something about Maggie, despite her wild colour sense, which made them feel safe.

Almost as soon as the story was told, the bus arrived. Maggie watched it stop, sighed and dug deep in her bag. She produced her bus pass. 'I can't let you two go off on your own. I may not be more responsible than you, but I am older.'

'Oh, good!' exclaimed Poppy, and even Will, who had never met her before, seemed pleased, although he did whisper to Poppy, 'Does she always dress like a London bus?'

As Poppy, Will and Maggie sped towards Paddington Station, Angel stood at a bus stop further back along the same road. The trouble was, Gus was there too and Angel hadn't told Gus what he was up to.

'Hey there, son. Sure you're going in the right direction?'

Gus was smoking, which surprised Angel until he realised it was one of those artificial cigarettes that light up when puffed. 'Didn't know you smoked,' said Angel, to change the subject.

'Don't. Didn't know your school was in this direction.'

'It isn't.' So, like Poppy and Maggie, Angel decided to tell Gus where he was going.

Gus thought hard and his wrinkled face wrinkled even more. 'So you're helping your friend Poppy. That's good. Only problem is, you're taking a bigger risk than she is. You've been in trouble before and this wouldn't look good in court.' He ticked off on his fingers, 'Skiving off school. Helping an escaping prisoner...'

Angel interrupted him. 'We're helping her dad to go back to prison! We're stopping him escaping!'

'Hmm. The courts might not see it that way. It's the sort of thing they think best left to the police.'

'But the feds will never catch him! And he'll be off in Ireland dealing drugs and doing no end of harm!'

'True. True.' Gus thought more, rubbing his hand over the top of his head so it looked more like a bristly white brush than ever. 'I'll tell you what. I'd better come with you. At least I can do a bit of talking if you get in a tight corner. Can't have my best left footer land up in clink.'

So Angel and Gus got on the bus and they sped along to Paddington Station.

Jude was also on a bus. Curious to see where Poppy and Maggie were going, she had followed them at a distance and seen them meet Will before getting on a bus. More curious than ever, she ran to the bus stop and caught the bus immediately behind theirs.

Of course, she didn't know where they were going, but she reckoned that she would easily spot that extraordinary woman's glaring red dress when she got off.

At least, Jude thought, they didn't have that no-good Angel with them!

Paddington Station is encased by iron arches and curved glass. At rush hour, when thousands of travellers are surging in every direction, it's a noisy and confusing place.

Poppy, Will and Maggie went from the bus stop to the main entrance and stood staring distractedly around them.

'What if we see your dad?' asked Will, as two large men with brief cases squashed him against a wall.

'We confront him at once,' shouted Poppy, as

a small man wheeling a large bicycle came between them.

'What if he runs away from us?' asked Will, as two girls swung their handbags over his head.

'Chase him!' called Poppy, as someone right beside her started yelling into his mobile.

'Chase him,' echoed Maggie doubtfully, and her eyes swept the crowds of people.

Outside the station, Jude had just got off the bus, but it was the wrong stop. She'd seen a woman in a red coat get off the bus ahead and realised too late that it wasn't Maggie. Looking round, she saw where she was and guessed that Poppy and the others must be heading for Paddington Station. The trouble was, instead of being at the station entrance, she faced a street full of road works. She'd have to walk all the way round to the other side of the station. She thought about heading back to school, but none of the buses were going in the right direction.

'It's all Poppy's fault,' she said to herself, and started trekking round to the other side.

Angel and Gus got off at the right bus stop.

Gus said, 'Last time I was at Paddington Station there was a bomb alert and the whole place was evacuated. The evacuation took so long, we'd have all been blown sky-high if the bomb had gone off.'

Soon they were at the same entrance where Poppy, Will and Maggie had been waiting, but there was no sign of them now.

'What's the plan?' asked Gus.

'We're all meeting here,' said Angel

'Where?' asked Gus.

Angel thought about this. He stood back a bit as commuters streamed past. 'I don't know,' he admitted.

'Nothing ventured, nothing gained,' said Gus, and they pushed into the station together.

Jude was still walking round the outside of the station. She was hot, flustered and her normally well-behaved hair had come out of its band. She wondered what she would do if she couldn't find

Poppy and Will. She didn't feel like going tamely back to school.

She turned into the station and suddenly saw, not far ahead of her, a back she knew very well: Angel! Of course – he had to be involved in anything forbidden that Poppy and Will were doing.

However, there was no sign of Poppy or the others. At Angel's side was a brown, wrinkled person with standing-up white hair. The question was, whether to approach Angel. After all, she'd forbidden Poppy ever to talk about him. She wished she didn't feel so lost and alone.

'Hi, Angel!'

Angel turned round and when he saw Jude, assumed a relaxed slouch. She supposed he was trying to look cool. 'Hi. Didn't know you were coming on the chase too.'

Jude frowned. She wasn't going to admit she had no idea what he was talking about. 'Last minute thing,' she said – which was true enough.

The old man took a step towards her. 'Introductions, Angel?'

'This is Gus,' said Angel. 'She's Jude.'

Not very polite, thought Jude, but it would do. 'I'll come with you,' she said firmly, in case they disappeared.

'We're looking for Angel's friend Poppy,' explained Gus.

'Me too,' said Jude.

❧

Poppy was standing with Will and Maggie at the barrier to the Heathrow Express. Their mood wasn't good. Maggie had just announced that her legs were swollen up like balloons and Will kept looking at his watch and saying unhelpful things like, 'This is your fifty-eight-minute countdown to aeroplane take-off and departure of Person F.'

'We've only been waiting ten minutes,' pointed out Poppy, 'and we can't go without Angel because he's got all the money.'

'I'm glad someone's got money,' grumbled Maggie, who would definitely have preferred to be somewhere else. 'This Heathrow Express costs a fortune, I'm told, although I've never been on it. Where did Angel get all his money, then?' Will was about to tell her but she interrupted him: 'No. No. I don't want any more information.'

'If we miss this train,' said Will, looking at the

electronic notice board, 'we'll have fifteen minutes before the next one. Which will give Person F a good chance of escape.'

'When did you start this Person F thing?' complained Poppy irritably.

'You never know who's listening,' replied Will in a dignified voice. 'We *are* on a secret mission.'

Poppy was about to argue, when she caught sight of Angel.

'Angel. Over here!' she shouted, and waved until Will whispered fiercely, 'Sshh! Do you want your dad to see you!'

'Then we can catch him,' she retorted.

'But if he sees us first before we see him, he'll run away, and then we'll never catch him,' said Will.

'And there's Gus,' hissed Maggie in a loud stage whisper. 'But who's that girl with them? She looks hot enough to fry an egg on.'

Poppy and Will peered through the crowds.

'Did you invite Jude?' Will asked accusingly.

'No,' answered Poppy. 'We're scarcely on speaking terms.'

Meanwhile, Angel had spotted them and led over Gus and Jude.

'Any sign of Big Frank?' he asked.

'No sighting of Person F,' answered Will conspiratorially. 'Which means we proceed with immediate effect to conveyance B.H.E.'

'What's that?' Angel looked bewildered.

'Heathrow Express,' explained Will. 'Our second conveyance after the bus, therefore "B". H. E. is obviously Heathrow Express.'

'Cool,' agreed Angel, although he still wore a wondering look.

'Got the wherewithal, have you?' asked Will.

'Where with what?' asked Angel.

'Money,' whispered Will.

While Will and Angel worked on planning, Poppy confronted Jude.

'Whatever are you doing here?'

'I might ask the same of you,' answered Jude spikily. 'Paddington Station on a school day? Seeing you disappear round the corner like that. I was curious, wasn't I.'

'So you followed us,' said Poppy crossly.

'Yes.' Jude answered defiantly, before adding in a softer voice, 'I wanted to come with you.'

'But you said you didn't want anything more to do with Angel, and he is part of it.'

'I felt left out,' said Jude, deciding to be honest.

'But you wanted to be left out,' insisted Poppy. 'And I felt left out when you went off with Amber, but I didn't follow you.'

Jude looked ashamed, which was a first as far as Poppy was concerned. 'Sorry,' she said. 'I was frightened about what Angel might get up to. I'm not brave like you. I really am sorry.'

Poppy was wondering whether it was worth the bother of forgiving her, when Gus interrupted, 'So are we getting on this train or not?'

'Yes. Yes,' said Will fussily. 'We really must catch this H.E. or we might miss Person F altogether.'

So they all hurried to the platform and stepped into the nearest carriage, which happened to be First Class.

'Who's Person F?' asked Jude, but no one heard her as they moved up the train, avoiding people, cases, bags and boxes.

Eventually they found seats so that they all could sit together. Jude seemed to have become one of the party.

'Ooh,' Maggie breathed out a sigh of release as she eased off her shoes. 'Anyone got a pair of feet to lend me?'

'Tickets, please,' demanded the smart ticket

collector lady advancing down the aisle.

Everybody (except Jude who didn't know about Mr Moneybags) looked at Angel expectantly.

Chapter Twenty-one

Angel, frowning a little as if weighted with responsibility, reached into his trouser pocket. Since his trouser pockets were zipped and buttoned, this took a while.

'No, man!' His hand came back empty.

Five pairs of eyes gazed anxiously at him. The ticket collector waited, tapping her pen on her machine.

'It's gone, hasn't it,' exclaimed Angel.

Anxiety changed to horror. Even Maggie stopped rummaging in her bag.

'Now, son.' Gus sounded firm. 'Put your hand in deeper.'

Angel reached down with his hand again, and this time came up smiling. 'Just joking!' he shouted, waving a roll of notes over his head.

Nobody smiled back.

'So that's two adults and four children,' said the ticket collector disapprovingly, as if they were spoiling the calm of her train – which they were, since a lot of the passengers were staring their way and whispering.

'Return,' said Gus.

'I didn't think you were flying anywhere,' said the ticket collector snarkily. 'That'll be one hundred and thirty-six pounds.'

'Daylight robbery!' exclaimed Maggie.

'No problem.' Angel peeled off the notes with a flourish. 'Fifty, one hundred, one hundred and twenty, one hundred and forty. Change, please.'

The ticket collector continued to look cross, 'Haven't you got a card?'

'Does he look as if he's got a card?' asked Gus, and they all laughed. The idea of Angel with a credit card was just silly.

'Don't you accept real money?' put in Maggie. 'At those prices, I'd accept anything I could get.'

So the ticket collector found four pound coins and handed them over. Then, with some reluctance, she printed out the tickets.

'Thank you, madam.' Angel bowed with exaggerated politeness.

Once she had gone, Maggie produced a huge bag of toffees. 'I wasn't going to get them out while that stuck-up *mademoiselle*, excuse my French, was here.'

Poppy took a toffee like the others, but she was not happy. The day was beginning to feel like a holiday outing rather than a serious mission. 'So what's our plan?' she asked in an intense voice.

Will sprang to attention. 'Disembarkation at Terminal One, proceed in a group to Departure Lounge, ascertain Check-in Desk for Departure to Belfast, separate to cover points of possible Person F escape…'

'What's all this in normal speak?' interrupted Maggie.

'A lot of walking,' smiled Gus.

'Oh, no!' groaned Maggie.

'Please, Maggie,' wailed Poppy.

'Don't worry, love,' Maggie patted Poppy's hand. 'I'll draw on hidden resources.'

'Very well hidden,' commented Gus.

By now, Jude had some idea of what was going on and decided to risk a question.

'Is Person F Big Frank?'

'Only in Will's weird speak,' said Angel.

'At least Will's got a plan,' said Poppy. 'I want to make it clear that I never asked Jude to come.'

'Now, now, Poppy.' Maggie wagged her finger

which was covered with rings, including one the size of an egg, at Poppy. 'She's given you a home, hasn't she?'

'I am sorry. I'm so sorry I've been so mean lately,' Jude appealed to Poppy. 'I promise I'll be different from now on. I honestly want to help. But tell me, why are we chasing Big Frank? Isn't he in prison?'

So then Poppy had to explain all over again about her dad's plan to escape and fly to Ireland, and how they were going to get him back before anyone noticed he was missing.

'Oh, that's terrible! And then he'd be thrown into that prison on the top of a rock again. I'll never forget how frightening it was!' Jude looked so upset that suddenly, Poppy found she could forgive her. Jude would never be easy, but at least they could be friends.

'That's right,' said Maggie approvingly as the two girls hugged, while Angel and Will looked the other way.

They were all diverted as the train entered a long tunnel. Then there was an announcement: 'Terminal One. All passengers for Terminal One. Please make sure to take all baggage with you. Any baggage left unattended may be disposed of.'

'Blown up,' said Will cheerily as they got off.

They were faced by a choice of silver tunnels along which the other passengers were scurrying, most pulling cases or pushing trolleys.

'I wish I was a case,' groaned Maggie. 'Then you could put me on a trolley.'

'We'll bring up the rear,' said Gus consolingly, and put his arm over hers. The children set off at a run, leaving them far behind.

'That's a lift, isn't it?' Will, who was panting heavily, slowed down. 'Aeroplanes can't take off from underground.' Angel, of course, didn't pant or even seem out of breath.

They all gathered round the lift doors in company with ten grown-ups, eight small children and twenty-five cases.

In the distance they saw Gus and Maggie steadily approaching.

Will looked at his watch. 'We're going to be late.'

'Stop being so negative!' exclaimed Poppy crossly.

The lift doors opened and grown-ups, children and cases crowded in. Poppy, Angel, Will and Jude were crushed in with them. Jude ended up sitting on top of a large box whose owner glared at her, hissing angrily in a language she didn't understand.

'Sorry,' she said, 'There was nowhere else.' His hiss turned into a growl and she gave up.

The lifts opened. Passengers streamed out and, to her horror, Jude saw that the large box had been balanced across a pushchair and inside the pushchair was a sleeping baby.

'I nearly squashed a baby!' she exclaimed to Poppy.

'Concentrate on the matter in hand,' replied Poppy, sounding rather like Will.

Will, holding a piece of paper which seemed to be covered in lists, was peering round anxiously.

'Where's Angel gone? The whole point of having a group of us is so that we can cover all possible areas of exit.'

'There are Gus and Maggie,' said Jude, pointing to another lift just opening.

Meanwhile Poppy was looking around frantically. She was sure that at any moment she'd see the tall figure of her dad and then she would have to confront him. What would she say? 'We've come to turn you in, unless you promise to get back to wherever you came from!' That sounded extremely aggressive. Or should she be more loving and daughterly? 'Oh my darling dad, for me your beloved Pops, please,

please turn yourself in!' That sounded totally unconvincing. Perhaps a lower-key approach? 'Your time is up…' But that sounded like calling in a boat on the Serpentine.

'Hey, dreamer!' Angel had come up silently the way he did, and stood beside her. 'I've checked on the flight. Nine-thirty, but delayed half an hour. He's not in sight anywhere downstairs. But we need to check all the shops carefully.'

'I don't think he's much of a one for shopping,' said Poppy doubtfully.

'He might need a razor. Then there's an upper floor of bars and restaurants.'

Poppy tried to look calmly at the scene in front of her. It was one vast space, L-shaped, with check-in desks down one side. As Angel said, there were stairs leading to an upper balcony.

They were joined by Gus and Maggie with Will and Jude tagging along behind.

'I don't know what people will think,' grumbled Maggie, 'with all these kids in school uniform running around an airport on a school day.'

'They'll think you and I are in charge, Madam Maggie, supervising a school project.' Gus smiled comfortingly.

'Will they now!' Maggie seemed pleased at this and handed out another round of toffees, while Angel filled them in with the results of his recce.

'OK.' Will ticked his sheet of paper. 'I'll go and stand by the departure gate.'

'And I'll go to Boots,' said Jude. 'I'm very good in chemists.'

'Of course, I'm your secret weapon.' Gus stared at the ground thoughtfully. 'I'm the only one of you Big Frank, sorry, Person F, won't recognise.'

'That's quite true,' said Poppy eagerly, 'Why don't you come up to the balcony with Angel and me. You can go ahead and spot him.'

'What about me?' asked Maggie, sounding offended.

'We need you on that nice chair in that nice café over there,' suggested Gus. 'If you see him you can wave your handkerchief – otherwise, you're a central meeting point.'

'*Allez-y*!' cried Will.

'What's that?' asked Maggie suspiciously. 'Is it a rude word?'

'No,' Will laughed. 'It's French for "Let's go!"'

With a great deal of Allez-y-ing they split up and set off for their target positions, as Will called them.

Poppy, Angel and Gus headed for the stairs to the upper balcony. At the top, Gus investigated a café immediately in front of them.

While he was waiting for Gus, Angel hung over the railings to the floor below. 'Just look at Maggie, man!' Poppy came to join him. 'Like an empress!' Maggie had pulled her chair into the main thoroughfare and settled her bag on her spread knees. In her hand she held a yellow handkerchief.

'Well, she might miss seeing my dad,' said Poppy, 'but he'd never miss her!'

'He'll probably be in too much of a state to remember her.'

'If only she wasn't in red!'

'He'll think she's a sitting-down pillar box,' laughed Angel.

Gus returned. ''Nothing there except bad coffee and hoards of silly people.'

Poppy tried not to be irritated that Angel and Gus were clearly enjoying themselves.

'Who's that?' she cried out abruptly, her stomach lurching. A big man had come out of a café further down and gone on ahead of them.

'Where? Where? '

'I don't know.' Poppy felt faint. She swayed a little.

'I've lost him. It might not have been him at all. I only saw his back.' She realised that she'd never expected to spot her dad so quickly. In fact she hadn't even been sure they'd find him.

Gus steadied her with a hand under her arm. 'Was he pulling a case?'

'No. I don't think so. I'm not sure. There're so many people and I couldn't see his hair…'

'You'd always recognise your dad,' said Angel firmly. 'Do you think it was him?'

Poppy took a deep breath. Of course it had been him. Her body, now all hot inside, told her so.

'Yes,' she said.

'Cheers!' Angel gave her a high five – which Poppy missed.

'Action stations,' said Gus. 'I'll go on ahead. If he's sitting down, I'll get near him. Even sit at the same table. Poppy, you stay here to block his exit this end. Angel, go down and round to the staircase at the other end of the balcony to make sure he doesn't escape that way. Let Maggie know we've spotted him.'

Angel dashed off and Poppy, heart thudding, watched the small figure of Gus threading his way between the crowds of people and the cafes. He had pulled on a luminous yellow cap which made him easy to follow. At each café he disappeared for a moment or two, then re-emerged, obviously having found nothing, and continued on his way. Soon he was nearly at the end. Perhaps, thought Poppy nervously, Big Frank had slipped away down the stairs before Angel took up guard.

Then the yellow cap turned to face her. She couldn't see Gus's expression clearly, but he was mouthing something. His arm came up and his hand waggled in what could only be a thumbs-up. Poppy's heart beat even faster. The yellow cap disappeared again.

'He's not in the chemist.' The whisper came from Jude behind her.

'He's up there somewhere,' Poppy whispered back, although her dad certainly couldn't hear them.

'Have you seen the police?' mouthed Jude.

'No.'

'Armed,' hissed Jude, her eyes popping. 'I'll show you.'

They moved to the edge of the balcony and looked over. Two policemen, in black with body armour and carrying serious guns, stood below.

'I don't know whether that's good or bad,' murmured Poppy fearfully. 'I don't believe that they're looking for Dad – not yet – so we can use them to threaten him. But if he does something stupid…' She broke off. 'Oh, Jude, I do love him, but I wish he could be a bit more like other people's dads.'

Jude nodded sympathetically. 'He always was larger than life.'

'Is.' Poppy sighed. 'Gus may be chatting him up now. Let's get a bit closer.'

So the two girls cautiously moved forward until they could see where Gus had gone in. It was like a pub, dark with orange lights and a long bar down one side. It was filled mostly with men sitting at small tables drinking beer.

'Beer at this hour of the morning!' whispered Poppy.

Then she saw her dad – and he was sitting with Gus – talking! They each had a large beer in front of them. 'Do you see that!'

'I see that!' Jude was equally gobsmacked. 'You know, you've got to confront him some time. Perhaps this is the moment.'

'Do you think?' Poppy's heart began to beat in double time. What if it all went wrong and those police with their guns got involved? She guessed that an escaping prisoner would be taken very seriously, even if he was in an open prison. She looked at Jude, then back to her dad, his hair glowing in the orange lights.

'Let's get Angel up here', she suggested.

'What if your dad does a runner?'

'That's true.' Poppy knew she was playing for time.

She made up her mind. 'OK.' She stepped forward with Jude just behind her.

At once a tall man wearing a smart black shirt barred her way, 'You girls on your own?'

'Say it's your dad,' hissed Jude.

'My dad's in there...' began Poppy.

But at that moment, to her horror, she saw Big Frank glance at his watch and leap to his feet. He headed towards another exit some way from where they were standing.

'Please!' she stuttered. But the tall man's bulk was planted squarely in front of her.

'You two lost, are you?'

'My dad. He's leaving. Please.'

He shifted his head slightly but didn't look over his shoulder. Poppy saw that Gus was following Big Frank.

'Dad!' she shrieked. 'It's me! Poppy! Don't go! Dad! Dad!'

But Big Frank was already at the top of the stairs.

Chapter Twenty-two

Angel was standing guard at the bottom of the stairs. Behind him, Will was lurking near the departure gate.

Angel was watching the two policemen, who were advancing slowly. He was just wondering whether he'd like to be a policeman and carry a gun when he grew up when, above the airport din, he heard Poppy's shriek.

Luckily, the feds didn't. Trying not to attract their attention, Angel moved to the middle of the bottom stair. From there he could at least try to stop anyone coming down. Several people passed by him – a family, a single woman, two men together.

Angel glanced nervously at the policemen. In a second they would be level with him. He looked back up the stairs – and there was Big Frank coming down fast.

There was no help for it,

'I'm Angel, Poppy's friend.' He was going to add, 'We met in prison', when he glimpsed the policemen who were very near now.

Frank was about to brush past Angel when he stopped abruptly, his eyes widening. He'd just noticed the policemen. He hesitated. Then for the first time he looked at Angel, although he didn't seem to recognise him.

'I need your help,' he said.

'What?'

'I want you to go up to those policemen and ask about their guns. Men like that love to show off their fire power. I'll pay you. Look, twenty pounds.' He took out a note.

'I don't need money.' Angel felt the roll in his pocket while considering what to do. Where was Poppy? And Gus? And Jude? He glanced around. The feds had stopped a few yards from him and were chatting to each other in a relaxed way.

Big Frank still hesitated. Angel supposed he was worried in case the police were looking out for him.

Frank glanced anxiously at his watch. He was sweating heavily, his shirt blotched and his face red. Not cool, thought Angel. Just at that moment Poppy appeared, slid down the stairs, and grabbed her father's arm.

'Dad! It's Poppy! We've come to rescue you!

Dad, that man up there wouldn't let me go and I thought I'd lost you!' She burst into tears.

Frank's face was frozen in amazement as Poppy gabbled on. He looked so dumb that Angel nearly started laughing. But as Poppy went on crying, Frank became panicky again. He tried to comfort her, but his gaze kept flickering across to the policemen. Clearly, he still hoped to do a runner.

'If you try and leave,' gulped Poppy through her tears, 'we'll tell those police.'

'Yeah. Those officers with automatics,' added Angel emphatically.

Big Frank took a step forward as if he might hit Angel. 'You wouldn't do that!'

'Yes, we would.' Angel didn't budge. 'And behind Poppy there's Gus and Jude, and behind me there's Will and Maggie. One of us will shop you if you're not careful – you need to think about getting back on your train and going back to work. It's your only hope. You remember me. I'm Angel. My dad was in prison with you. He's been in and out of jail all my life and I know, if you mess up now, you'll never turn it round. We're giving you a chance, man.'

At first Frank's anger and desperation seemed to be mounting, but by the end of Angel's speech there was a change. His shoulders slumped and he let go of Poppy. Taking a step towards Angel, he muttered, 'I remember you now. How did a boy like you learn to talk like that?'

'School of hard knocks,' said Angel.

At last Gus and Jude had appeared and were coming down the stairs.

'Hi,' said Jude brightly.

Big Frank seemed beaten. Then he spotted Gus.

'You were sitting at my table,' he said, accusingly. 'You talked so much, I nearly missed my plane.'

'And now you have missed it,' said Gus in a pleased voice.

'I suppose so.' Big Frank sighed and patted Poppy's shoulder. 'I was going to make her rich.'

'I don't want to be rich,' said Poppy, sniffing. 'I don't want you in Ireland doing bad things and going back to Castlerock Prison for years. I want you home! And I want Mum home, and I want…'

Angel hastily interrupted, 'Hey, let's tell Will and Maggie we've got Person F.' He turned to Frank. 'We have got you, haven't we?'

Frank looked past them all to where the two policemen were still chatting. He nodded in their direction. 'Better you than them.'

'Just what I thought,' said Angel, smiling. 'I might just check out their guns.'

Frank didn't smile back. He gave Angel a sharp look. 'It was at Heathrow I was arrested the first time.' He clapped Angel hard on the shoulder. 'How about a celebration drink?'

'Drink?' Gus stepped up to Frank, and, although he came scarcely to his shoulder, there was something steely about him. Angel, watching, thought he was dealing with Frank just like he did with the boys at the football club when they got out of line. 'You've done your drinking for today. Now it's back to work.'

Big Frank stood his ground for a couple of seconds, as Angel had often seen the boys do, then walked down the final three steps.

'Fine firepower you have there, gentlemen,' he said, as he passed the policemen.

The men looked up in a bored way. The biggest, who was as tall as Frank, shifted his gun from one side of his chest to the other. Then they noticed Frank's escort of two girls and one boy in various school uniforms and an old man in a baseball cap.

'All yours, are they?'

'Thank the good Lord, no. Just the one with the hair.' Frank was recovering his bravado.

The policeman smiled not very nicely. 'Called you Carrots, did they?'

Frank's face went a deeper shade of red. 'They didn't dare!' He clenched his fists.

Catching sight of Poppy's agonised face, Angel quickly intervened. 'Over here, Will.'

Will came up. 'Uhm. Nice to see you, sir,' he gulped and held out his hand so that Frank could hardly avoid shaking it.

The two policemen stepped back, although keeping a wary eye on Frank.

Man, is he his own worst enemy, thought Angel, before realising with an inward smile that that was just what people used to say about him.

'Hi, girls and boys!' Maggie chose this moment to make her appearance. Her sit-down seemed to have restored her exuberant spirit. 'Well, here's the big man himself! Oh dear, what a dance you've led us.'

As Big Frank tried to remember whether he knew this mad lady, the policemen decided they were looking at a collection of crazies and moved off.

'I'm Maggie,' announced Maggie. 'Poppy's friend. We came to see you at, er –' she gave a polite little cough to show she was avoiding the word prison – 'Churchill House.'

'Oh yes, it slipped my memory for a moment.' Frank was still quailing at the red apparition.

'I don't know how anyone could forget Maggie,' Jude whispered to Poppy.

Poppy smiled wanly, 'I don't think my dad's quite himself.'

Angel thought how often he'd had the same idea about his dad, until he'd finally realised that the dad he saw was the real dad, good and bad mixed. Bad, mostly, in his dad's case.

'Now we're all gathered,' said Gus, holding up his watch, 'we'd better move off.' He looked at Big Frank meaningfully.

Will nudged Angel. 'There isn't another flight to Belfast till the afternoon. He'd have to buy a new ticket even to go through to Departures. I asked. On the other hand,' he continued, eyes gleaming, 'he might just abscond for the thrill of it!'

'Yeah.' Abscond was quite a word, but Angel got the hang of it. You couldn't trust Big Frank to hold a single course of action for very long. The sooner they were on the train, the better.

The airport was more crowded than ever as they headed out. To get to the lift, they had to pass several exits to the bright world outside.

At the third exit, Big Frank surprised everyone by going so close to the doors that they opened automatically, and he was outside. Angel and Gus dashed out to join him.

'Just sniffing the air.' Frank put his nose up to the sky with an innocent expression. 'It's a fine day out here!'

Angel smiled. Frank really was like a naughty little boy. But Gus said firmly, 'You can sniff the air on Paddington Station. It's very high-class air, I'm told.'

Poppy joined them, anxiously clasping her dad's arm. 'Come on, Dad. You've already been away hours. What if someone misses you?'

Big Frank allowed himself to be led, mumbling jovially, 'He went like a lamb to the slaughter.'

'I bet he had more than one drink in the bar,' Will whispered to Angel. The two boys nodded wisely.

It was a relief to get down below to the train platform where there was nowhere to run. It was darkish, of course, and there were so many people that Big Frank could easily have hidden, but he seemed intent on entertaining everyone now.

'You are a dazzling lady!' He told Maggie, 'I thought so before, when you honoured my humble abode with a visit, and I think so now. My eyes swivel towards you in admiration. You are, without an atom of doubt, the queen of my heart!'

Maggie seemed pleased at his attentions and directed a large wink at Poppy as if to say, 'Your dad's in fine form. Let's keep him going.'

He was still making silly jokes when they got on the train. Angel was 'the angel of wisdom and light', Will 'the sword of truth', Jude 'the shade of peace'.

There was a slightly tricky moment when he realised they were on a train, not the Tube. 'Why do you want to waste your money on such an expensive means of travel?' complained Frank.

'It's quicker,' answered Gus.

After that he settled in a seat with Poppy and seemed content for several minutes until, just after the ticket inspector had been – as if the sight of his money going in her direction had jerked his memory – he began a kind of worried grunting.

Eventually, he exclaimed, 'You kids don't know the danger you're putting me in, sending me back!'

Angel, who was sitting across the aisle from him, asked, 'Danger? What danger? We're saving you from danger.'

Frank snorted contemptuously. 'Who do you think gave me the wad of bills in my pocket? The prison service? Probation?'

'Ssshh, Dad,' implored Poppy.

Gus turned round from the seat in front and Maggie rolled her eyes heavenwards.

Big Frank ignored them all and carried on. 'The gentlemen who gave me those bills aren't going to be overjoyed if I miss the Belfast flight. I'm a key part of their operation. Planning took months. Messed up. Mucked up. And here I am sitting with a bunch of kids and two weirdos going back where I came from. Upfront money still in my pocket. How do you think those gentlemen will feel? Happy? Would you say happy?'

Several passengers in the carriage turned round.

'How will they know?' asked Poppy, anxiously.

'They'll know all right when I don't turn up to do my bit of the plan.' He rubbed his face furiously. 'If it comes to that, they've probably had someone watching me at the airport. They leave nothing to chance, those thugs.' He raised his voice. 'Might be in this very carriage watching me.'

'Sshh, Dad,' repeated Poppy.

Angel was beginning to see what Big Frank meant. The sort of men he'd been dealing with were not going to let him get off free when he not only had their money, but had also scuppered their plans. They *were* dangerous.

'Could have been one of those so-called police with the big guns,' continued Frank. 'They seemed peculiarly interested in us.'

'They didn't, Dad,' protested Poppy weakly.

'And now you want me to hang around a station where anyone could bump me off, no questions asked?'

'What's he going on about?' Gus, who couldn't quite get the drift from where he was sitting, asked Angel.

'Revenge. Vengeance,' Angel ran a finger across his throat. 'He thinks he's in danger from his mates. Ex-mates. The ones he was working for.'

'I see.' Gus looked grim.

'Yeah,' agreed Angel. 'He's not wrong.'

Meanwhile Big Frank's ranting had changed to dejected silence. When Poppy said hopefully, 'We'll protect you,' he smiled ironically.

'You kids are going back to school out of the way. I'll think of something. Don't worry.' He attempted a smile, although he couldn't resist adding, 'I'd be better off back in Castlerock.'

They were only a few minutes from Paddington Station now. As Angel explained the problem to Jude and Will, the tension grew.

'You mean, it's really serious?' asked Jude, eyes wide.

'Think guns,' said Angel. 'Punishment.'

He'd scarcely finished the word when there was a violent shrieking of brakes, sudden and sharp enough to cause people standing up to fall over each other and bags to fall off the racks.

The train, screaming in protest, came to a halt.

Twenty-three

'I'm out of here!'

Big Frank pushed his way through the tumbling passengers and made for the door. The others were too slow, but Angel followed him.

Frank glanced behind him. 'Emergency exit,' he said, 'before they find me.' Fear seemed to have made Frank quite agile, for such a heavy man. They were out on the track quickly, and only a hundred metres ahead of them was the station.

'If we can get there before they see me,' panted Frank, 'I can slip on a train and get back to work. No one suspects a man with a J-cloth and rubber gloves.'

Angel couldn't help admiring the way Frank ran, skipping along beside the railway lines. He was hard put to keep up. Behind them, their train was still stationary but they had to look out for other trains coming into the station. Not much fun to be flattened under two ton wheels.

'Stay with me,' said Frank, as they took a quick

breather. 'Then you can tell Poppy and the rest I'm safe.'

'Safe' wasn't a good word, for at that moment a gunshot rang out.

Frank didn't even turn his head. 'Don't look. Just keep running. We're well ahead.'

It was like the movies. But Angel wished he was watching it, not part of it.

Gus was trying to calm Maggie who'd thrown a small fit, murmuring, 'My, my, my,' while holding her bag protectively in front of her face .

'Why's the train stopped? wailed Jude. The same question was being asked in many different languages by all the other travellers in the carriage:

'*Pourquoi le train s'est arrêté?*'

'*¿Por qué el tren se detuvo?*'

'*Miksi juna pysähtyi?*'

'*Dlaczego pociag zatrzymanl?*'

'And where has Dad gone?' cried Poppy. She was nearly in tears. They had been so near to getting him safely back to work.

'And Angel,' added Will, sounding aggrieved.

'He's gone too.'

'I guess they're running away,' said Gus in a matter-of-fact voice. He turned to Poppy. 'I'm afraid your dad was right. His new friends don't like the fact he's decided not to help them.'

'So they pulled the emergency chain,' said Jude slowly, as if she couldn't quite believe what she was saying. 'And now they're after Big Frank.'

Maggie put down her bag. 'It's very inconsiderate of them, leaving us stuck here in the middle of nowhere.'

'Actually, we're near the station.' Poppy pressed her face against the window.

'Can you see them?' asked Will excitedly.

'Not a sign.'

'It's all most annoy—' Maggie had just begun a new moan, when the carriage doors opened and two men dressed in black with hoods over their faces burst into the carriage.

They came in so suddenly and raced through so quickly that there was scarcely time to react. Then someone shouted, 'They've got guns!' And once more the cry was taken up in several languages:

'Sie habben Waffen!'

'Ils ont des armes!'

'Oni maja bron!'

At which point, half of the travellers threw themselves on the floor and the rest stood still and screamed, 'Ahhhhh!' 'Aieee!' or 'Help!' But by then the men had disappeared into the next carriage.

Gus patted Poppy comfortingly, 'Your dad and Angel are miles ahead of them. They might be at the station by now.'

Maggie, who had retired once more behind her bag, peered over the top and proclaimed loudly, 'Men are so stupid.'

At that moment there were two loud, popping sounds.

'Gunshots!' shouted a tall man, and no one said anything else in any language because they were listening too hard.

'They came from outside the train,' whispered Will.

It's surprising how fast you can run if there are men with guns chasing you. Angel thought he and Frank were going at top speed until they heard the bangs behind him – then they moved up into a whole new gear.

They were lurching like exhausted drunks when at last the end of the first platform appeared in front of them. They both put on a final spurt of speed and Frank gave Angel a hand up. On the next platform they could see six or seven station police advancing in a crouch. 'They must have heard the shots,' Angel panted.

'Hop on this train,' grunted Frank. 'Now!' The train was waiting for passengers on the other side of the platform. 'I don't want to be shot and I don't want to be picked up by the men in blue.'

The train was still only half-full. They walked through it quickly. Angel followed Frank closely, listening to his heavy breathing. He sounded like a steam train. Then he stopped so suddenly that Angel ran into his broad back.

With shaking hands, Frank pulled a bit of paper out of his pocket and unfolded it. 'My work timetable for today. Trains I'm supposed to clean.'

'Cheers,' stuttered Angel, still trying to get his breath back. 'So you were working at Paddington all along.'

Frank, frowning over the paper, ignored this. 'Eleven-fifteen,' he said. 'Platform Twelve. It should be in by now. '

Angel watched with surprise as Frank drew out an orange transport worker's vest from his other pocket, put it over his head and pulled it down.

'Do I look the part?'

'Sure.' Strange how that vest made him almost invisible. 'Pity you don't have a cap, though.'

'My hair, you mean. Stands out like a beacon.' Frank frowned. 'I'll flatten it with water. I'll tell you what, those killers won't like being met by a posse of police. Stupid of them to let off those shots.'

As Frank hurried off to the toilet, Angel thought how right he was. Once the shots had been fired, the feds had popped up out of nowhere.

Frank reappeared, his hair wet and subdued. 'Time to descend. Time of danger, so watch out.'

Cautiously they both got off the train. Angel immediately looked up.

'Isn't that a helicopter?'

They both stared as a helicopter came rapidly towards the end of the station, where it hovered.

'It's over our train,' said Frank.

'Quick work.' For once, Angel was impressed by the feds' efficiency.

'That'll scare them off.' Frank was more relaxed,

although the sweat ran off his face. 'You'd better bunk off. Enough risks for one day.'

'What about your cleaning stuff?'

'I gave it to my mate. He was going to cover for me if any questions were asked. He'll hand it over. What is it? Worried I'll do another runner?'

'It's Poppy,' replied Angel, feeling stupid. He was just a boy, wasn't he, trying to tell a grown man how to behave.

'What about Poppy?'

'She wants you home.' Angel felt even more stupid saying that.

But Frank looked pleased. 'Nice to be wanted. You know that.' He tapped the piece of paper he was still holding. 'And if you want to know where my mate is, it's all down here. Platform Eleven, next to mine. The Eleven-eighteen.'

Angel began to believe that Frank really *did* mean to finish the day's work before going back to Churchill House.

'I'll be off. Mustn't push my luck.' Frank took a step away, then turned back and patted Angel's shoulder.

'Thanks, mate. Say thanks to Poppy too. And the lot of them. You were right. Mine was a rotten plan. Tell Poppy I'll try and make a go of things.'

With that, he was off.

Angel watched his tall figure until it merged with the crowds. Wow, he thought. I do believe he'll get away with it. Then he thought, what I need is a cold drink…

⁂

The Heathrow Express gave a jerk and started moving again – very slowly, but moving. Poppy peered nervously out of the window. She feared she might see the dead bodies of her dad and Angel on the line. Instead she saw a helicopter.

Will and Jude craned over her to see it too.

'It's a police helicopter,' said Will excitedly.

Poppy made an effort to forget her worries about the dead bodies. 'Dad and Angel must have got to the station.'

'We're coming into Paddington.' Gus was admirably calm, In fact, he sounded just as if they had arrived back from a day trip and everything was normal.

The strangest thing was that everything did seem normal when they reached their platform and got off the train. There were a few more policemen around than usual, that was all.

'Angel will look after Dad,' said Poppy, more to herself than anyone else.

'Of course he will, love.' Maggie put her arm round Poppy. 'You wait. We'll see them in just a moment. If he'd been shot, or anyone else for that matter, there'd be ambulances everywhere. They can drive onto the concourse, you know.'

Jude and Will came to comfort her too.

'Your dad's a lucky man,' said Jude.

'Isn't there something called the luck of the Irish?' said Will. 'Big Frank's got it in triples.'

Poppy thought that he wasn't very lucky to spend years in prison. She didn't say anything, though, because they were only trying to be kind.

They walked slowly along to the front of the train. Around them were the other passengers who'd flown to Heathrow that day, all pulling cases or bags.

It was then that something even more surprising than anything else on that day of surprises happened to Poppy: she thought she saw her mother walking briskly ahead of her. The woman was dragging a large black suitcase with a purple ribbon round the handle.

It was so unlikely that Poppy didn't react at all

until Jude said, in a startled voice, 'Isn't that your mum up there?'

Poppy tried to laugh it off. 'We saw her off to Poland, remember?'

'It looks like her,' said Will, sidestepping to get a better view.

'I'd know my own mother, wouldn't I?' Poppy stopped walking and turned to them crossly.

'It's either her or a double,' insisted Jude.

'She didn't have a purple ribbon on her case. It was pink. I know, because I tied it on.'

'She could have changed it while she was in Poland.'

'I think you're both crazy!' Poppy shouted. 'It's my dad we're here for.'

Now Gus and Maggie, who'd walked ahead, came back to see what was going one.

'It's Poppy's mum,' said Will. 'She must have got off the same train as us. But Poppy's gone mad and won't believe it's her.'

'Where is she?' asked Gus. 'I'd like to meet her. I went to Poland once. For a fight. I lost, I'm sorry to say.'

'It's not my mum!' cried Poppy.

It is!' chorused Will and Jude. But when they tried

to point her out to Gus and Maggie, neither of them could see her any more.

'I told you, you were dreaming,' said Poppy, sounding pleased, although in her heart of hearts she so wanted it to be her mother, more than anything.

'She's gone ahead to the exit,' said Will.

'While we've been arguing,' added Jude.

'Well, we're going that way too,' said Maggie comfortably, and she gave Poppy a wink which Poppy was far too tense to return.

So they started walking again, more quickly, almost racing because Jude and Will wanted to be proved right and Poppy wanted to know whether it really was her mum. They were heading for the exit.

But they had only just reached the concourse of cafes and shops when Jude shouted, 'There she is!' And the woman heard her call and turned round.

Chapter Twenty-four

'Mum', said Poppy in a funny, strangled voice.

'Poppy,' whispered the woman.

'Mum', repeated Poppy more confidently.

Abandoning her suitcase, Poppy's mum flew towards her, arms wide. 'I wanted to surprise you,' she cried in her strong Polish accent.

'Well, isn't that nice!' exclaimed Maggie, coming from behind to see mother and daughter in a long, long hug.

'Told you so,' said Jude smugly. 'It's her mum back from Poland.'

'I didn't think it was the wicked witch come off her broomstick,' retorted Maggie. 'With a dad like hers, that girl needs a mum.'

'She must have been on the same train.' Will looked thoughtful. 'I wonder if she saw ... hmm...' He decided not to finish the sentence.

'So, my darling, darling Poppy, how did you know when to meet your mother?' Irena caught sight of

Jude and Will, 'And with your friends too. Hello, dear Jude and Will!' They got hugged too. 'I suppose my silly aunt rang you and tell. But the school to let you out, that is kind. I thought I meet you at the school gates but this is a wonderful miracle!' Poppy, Jude and Will gave each other meaningful looks and wondered if they should explain the miracle. Then, behind Poppy's mum, they saw Gus shaking his head. He was right. Much too complicated. Much better not.

'I still cannot believe such a perfect thing should happen.' Irena frowned perplexedly. 'The train it was terrible. Terrible. Full of men rushing along with guns. I thought I had come to the wrong country. Like bad Russia, not good England. And who are you?' she said suddenly, turning to Maggie. 'Your colour red is startling but full of good cheer.'

'I am Maggie.' She introduced herself in a rather stately manner. 'I am escorting these kids.'

'Oh, how kind!' exclaimed Irena again. She seemed overwhelmed. There were tears were in her eyes. She waved her hands and then hugged Maggie. 'How kind of the school to spare you!'

'And this is Gus.' Maggie extricated herself and pointed at Gus, who looked as if he'd like to retreat from all the emotion. 'He has come along for the ride!'

Gus bowed politely.

'Of course,' continued Maggie, who seemed on a roll, 'I will need to take the kids back to school as soon as possible. The headmaster made that very clear.' She lowered her voice, 'He can be extremely *difficile*, excuse my French.'

Despite the seriousness of everything – they still didn't know what had happened to Big Frank – Jude and Will had to stifle their giggles. The idea of Maggie as the school's choice for a responsible adult was just too funny. Even Poppy, who was keeping close to her mum in case she disappeared again, smiled.

But Irena was far too emotional and happy to question anything. 'Perhaps a very quick celebration drink before you take them away again?' she suggested.

'And why not,' agreed Maggie graciously. 'Lead on, my dear!'

So Irena and Poppy led the way, holding hands and staring into each other's faces as if trying to believe they really were together again.

They were discussing which café to choose when Irena took a little dancing step, 'Oh, look! Angel has come to meet me too! Why is he back-hanging?'

Poppy and the others followed her gaze, and there indeed was Angel, last seen running along the tracks behind Big Frank, now sitting in a café, coolly sipping a Coke.

'Angel!' called Poppy.

He hadn't seen them before and looked up with a big grin. Dad must be all right, thought Poppy. She glanced at her mum. Somehow she must warn Angel not to say anything about the day's events.

'Hi!' Hi!' Hi!' 'Hi!' The greetings took several minutes. Then, before Poppy could think what to say, Gus pronounced meaningfully to Angel, 'Irena's – so – glad – you – could – join – the – WELCOME PARTY.'

Angel hardly missed a beat. 'Yeah. And she must be glad too.' Now it was his turn to talk with deliberation. 'That Big Frank – is – WORKING – outside – prison – with NO PROBLEMS.'

Poppy saw Will and Jude nudge each other. So her dad was all right. Maybe he was even cleaning one of the trains behind them at this moment.

'Only good news.' Irena smiled ecstatically. 'My darling Poppy is with me and my darling husband is good and reliable and worthy-trust!'

At this description of Frank's good character, Jude and Will tried very hard not to catch each other's eye in case they laughed. The result was an explosive snorting sound.

'Oh,' said Irena, concerned. 'Something has gone down the throat.'

'A fly, yeah,' said Angel, who had stayed cool. 'More than one fly,' he added, as Will and Jude's spluttering grew.

'Sshh,' implored Poppy, going red. OK, her mum was a bit optimistic about her dad – but what was it they say: *love is blind* – and love is nice.

'Let's get those drinks.' Gus intervened.

So they put two tables together out on the forecourt and Irena waved a lot of notes about which seemed very generous, until Maggie gently pointed out half of them were Polish. Once that was settled and orders taken, Angel headed off to the bar inside.

'I'll help Angel bring them,' said Poppy quickly, because even though it was lovely to have her mum back, she still needed to know exactly what had happened to her dad.

We'll help too.' Will and Jude followed her.

The moment they were inside, all three turned on Angel.

'So how did he escape?'

'He did escape, didn't he?'

'We heard gunshots!'

'And a helicopter.'

'What happened, Angel?'

Angel took up a languid pose, hands in pockets. 'Nothing much, really. We ran. The bullets missed. We arrived at the station which was buzzing with police. We ducked into a stationary train where Big Frank changed into his cleaner's outfit. He checked which train he should be cleaning, and off he went. Oh, yes, he said thanks and that he was definitely going straight. That's it. As I said, nothing much.'

No one argued. At this point, 'nothing much' seemed the best possible outcome.

'Are you just chatting?' demanded the sharp-faced girl from behind the counter, 'Or are you planning to order?'

'Ordering!' shouted Angel, adding under his breath, 'Fat cow.'

'Sshh,' whispered Poppy.

'She reminds me of Eloise,' replied Angel, with the air of having the last word.

As they carried out the drinks and food, Will hung back and asked Angel under his breath, 'Do you mean that Big Frank is on the station cleaning a train at this moment?'

'Check. Why does it matter, man? He's doing the right thing, for once.'

'Suppose. But if he sees his long-lost wife…'

'Temptation. Yeah. Do a runner home.'

'He's such a show-off. Wouldn't like to be seen with mop and bucket.'

'He doesn't have a mop and bucket.'

'Rubber gloves, then. Womens' work.'

'Come on, boys!' Gus shouted from outside. 'We're dying of thirst while you two pass the time of day.'

'On our way!' Angel shouted back, before saying over his shoulder to Will, 'We'll just have to make sure they don't meet.'

At Paddington Station the way to the exit and the taxi rank which Poppy's mum needed, is along Platform Twelve.

When they reached it, Gus gallantly pulling Irena's suitcase, although it was nearly as tall as him, and the children walking ahead, Angel said in a low voice, 'Frank's working on this train waiting here. He'll probably come off it soon.'

'What? What?' Poppy grabbed Angel's arm.

'Your dad's cleaning this train.' He jerked his thumb. 'Leaves at eleven-fifteen, so he might pop out at any minute. Like, danger, man.'

For just a moment Poppy longed to jump aboard, check her dad was fine and give him a hug.

'We were worried it might be too much for him if he sees your mum,' said Will in an understanding voice.

'Oh, why do I have to have such a stupid dad!' cried Poppy petulantly, before subsiding and saying more sensibly, 'I do love him, but let's make certain they don't meet.'

'That's what we decided.'

'I could engage your mum in conversation,' suggested Will.

Jude, who'd been quiet up to now, gave a loud laugh. Will looked hurt.

'We'll just hurry her by,' said Poppy hastily.

'We'll keep train-side, then we can push Frank back in if he sticks out his head.' Angel seemed pleased at this prospect.

By now Irena, Gus and Maggie were approaching Platform Twelve, Irena skipping along happily, Gus bent over the case and Maggie puffing the way she did after any walk longer than a few yards.

Poppy came back to join them and immediately began talking animatedly on one side while Will and Angel took up sentinel duty on the side nearest the train. Jude danced ahead, pointing to the exit.

Irena seemed slightly bewildered but pleased at all the attention. 'I can't believe I stayed away so long,' she told Poppy tenderly.

Poppy felt like replying, 'Nor can I.' Instead, she took her mum's arm and said cheerily, 'Soon you'll be in a lovely taxi speeding home.'

Hardly had she finished speaking when a train door just in front of them was flung open.

'Person F!' shrieked Will.

At the same time, Angel launched himself in a rugby tackle.

Too late! Big Frank was among them. As surprised as them, he stood motionless. He was wearing his orange transport worker's vest and yellow plastic gloves. He clasped a large transparent bag filled with rubbish. His hair was still plastered to his head.

Everybody stared. Nobody could think of a thing to say.

Eventually Irena said in a wavering, uncertain voice, 'Frank, is that you?'

Nobody laughed.

Frank drew himself up so that he looked even bigger.

'Yes, Irena. It is me. And you are you.' He held up a yellow plastic hand and spoke with solemn emphasis. 'I am about God's business. You see in front of you a reformed sinner. One who has been tempted and has fallen but has now risen again. I am doing penance for my errors and until this unhappy time is over, I may not speak with you.'

'He'll get home leave soon,' whispered Angel to Poppy.

But now Frank was enjoying himself. 'I am humble. I am humiliated. But I am proud also. I have left evil behind me.'

'Oh Frank, Frank,' said Irena, who had probably heard this sort of declaration before because she didn't seem at all surprised. 'One kiss, and I'll be off. Such a treat to be seeing you and Poppy and all these beautiful children who came out especially to meet me.'

Frank kept his dignity while Irena reached up and kissed his cheek lovingly.

'Now I have to go,' he announced, and immediately strode past them and away to another platform.

'Phew!' exclaimed Will, which seemed an understatement.

'Oooph!' gasped Poppy, who'd been holding her breath up to that moment.

'Oh. Oh,' sighed Irena. 'My darling good Frank.' She dabbed at her eyes before giving Poppy a happy smile.

'Time for a taxi,' said Gus firmly, 'or these kids will be in real trouble at school.'

Reality came back with a nasty thump.

As soon as they had put Irena into the taxi – 'See you at the school gates!' she called from the window – the four children stared at each other miserably. They had to face the fact that they had skipped an entire morning's school.

'I can't think of one excuse.' Will sounded defeated.

'Obviously we can't tell the truth,' Jude said despairingly.

'At least we saved Big Frank,' said Poppy.

Angel didn't say anything. Missing a morning's school wasn't exactly news for him, although, since joining the football club, Gus had pressed on him the need for discipline and punctuality.

'You kids get too worried.' Maggie sounded untroubled. 'Don't forget, dinner ladies know all the ins and outs of the school. I'll get you there in time for your meal, then, when one of those dumb teachers asks where you were, you can say you had special permission to meet Poppy's mum off the train from Poland. Any difficulties, say it was from the headmaster himself. If they question it, say he must have forgotten to tell his secretary who therefore quite obviously couldn't tell them. Always good to blame the one at the top – particularly when it's a man.' Maggie gave a chortle.

'But that's lying.' Jude stared at Maggie, shocked.

'Yes, love,' agreed Maggie complacently. 'Anyone else got a better idea?'

Of course, no one did. Nor did they want to get in serious trouble.

'We really did meet my mum off the train,' pointed out Poppy, 'so it's only half a lie.'

'Even less than half,' added Will, 'because the headmaster might have given special permission if we'd asked him.'

'And if your teacher needs any further convincing,' said Maggie, still smiling, 'Tell her that Maggie the ex-dinner lady escorted you. They all love Maggie. I only left because my feet objected to all that standing. So now you've got even more truth to add to the mix!'

'Interesting,' said Will. 'I'd say the truth ratio has moved well above the lie ratio. What do you say, Jude?'

Jude was looking distinctly confused, but gave her permission for a lie which actually had more truth in it than lies.

Gus turned to Angel. 'And I'll take you into school myself, son. Can't risk problems for my champion left foot player.'

'Aren't you too busy?' Angel sighed theatrically. 'I need a day off after all that running.'

'There's the bus stop,' answered Gus, and pushed Angel on in front of him. 'If I pick you to play in the West London Junior Charity Cup you'll have to do a lot more running that that!'

'Hey. There's a chance, is there?'

'Always a chance, son. And give me that roll of money before we get to school.'

Poppy, Jude, Will and Maggie followed them to the bus stop.

Maggie smiled at their glum faces. 'Bit of a change,' she said sympathetically. 'Back to sitting in classrooms and being told what to do.' She nodded at Gus. 'But we know what you did and we respect you for it.'

Gus put a hand on Angel's shoulder. 'They talk about "elders and betters", but all my life I've found it the other way round. Give kids a chance, and they'll do better than us so-called grown-ups.'

Poppy, Angel, Jude and Will looked at their feet and wished they were anywhere else – although preferably not at school.

'You've embarrassed them,' said Maggie, smiling.

At last a bus came and they sprang into action.

'Kids' power!' shouted Will, clenching both fists.

'Girl power!' cried Jude.

'Sick...' chorused Angel.

'Quiet, you lot,' grumbled the driver, 'or I'll have you off my bus.'

'Great idea,' said Angel, making for the exit.

'Not so fast, young man.' Gus, who was already sitting down, grabbed Angel's arm and pulled him into a seat.

Poppy slid down beside him.

'It's strange,' she said thoughtfully, 'just how much looking after my mum and dad need.'

'Yeah.' Angel grinned. 'They're lucky having us kids to sort them out.'

Poppy's Hero is Rachel Billington's sixth novel for children and the sequel to *Poppy's Hero*. Rachel has been editor and regular contributor to *Inside Time*, the national newspaper for prisoners, since it was founded over twenty years ago. The experience has made her very aware of the difficulties facing the families of prisoners. She has lived in London all her life and has written often about the contrasting lives of the city where elegant terraces lead into cheerless estates. She has published twenty adult novels, including *The Missing Boy*, about a thirteen year old who runs away from home. She has four children and five grandchildren, all keen readers.

www.rachelbillington.com

POPPY'S HERO

Rachel Billington

When Poppy discovers her dad is in jail, she's furious – and wants him free. But the great escape she plans with her friend Will doesn't work out. Soon she's taking lessons from Angel, a hard-edged boy who knows all about the strange world of prisoners and their families – and up against the harsh realities, Poppy's questions really begin...

Sharply realistic, far removed from many stories on this theme, in which the accusation against a parent turns out to be an unjust and horrible mistake.
Books for Keeps

A well observed story inspired by the author's 20 years of prison work.
Independent on Sunday

LOOSE CONNECTIONS

Rosemary Hayes

Dad's abroad, Mum's ill in hospital, and Gran is looking after Jake. Or so everyone thinks. But soon Jake finds himself hiding a secret from his family, and the going gets tougher – until one day he meets a mysterious girl called Verity. Can discovering Verity's identity help him deal with his dilemma?

A deeply touching story, ... gently explores how a young boy deals with his granny's increasing confusion. How Jake sorts through the complications of his life is tenderly and thoughtfully explored.

Julia Eccleshare – Love Reading

SEA OF TEARS

Floella Benjamin

Jasmine is a typical British-born south London girl – smart, independent, plenty of attitude. But her parents are worried sick about the dangerous society in which they are raising their precious only daughter. They are determined to move the family to Barbados for a quieter, safer life. Jasmine is devastated – and when she starts school on the island she is bullied as an unwelcome outsider. All she can think about is finding a way to get back to Braitain – and that's when she spots the empty motor yacht. . .

'She writes with a sharp eye for details, with humour, with justice, with passion and with hope." –
Julian Fellowes, writer and actor